Pelican's LANDING

Gerri Hill

Bella
BOOKS

2015

Bella Books, Inc.
P.O. Box 10543
Tallahassee, FL 32302

First Bella Books Edition 2015

Editor: Medora MacDougall
Cover Designer: Judith Fellows
ISBN: 978-1-59493-450-6

Other Bella Books by Gerri Hill

About the Author

Gerri Hill has twenty-seven published works, including the 2013 GCLS winner *Snow Falls*, 2011 and 2012 GCLS winners *Devil's Rock* and *Hell's Highway*, and the 2009 GCLS winner *Partners*, the last book in the popular Hunter Series, as well as the 2012 Lambda finalist *Storms*. Hill's love of nature and of being outdoors usually makes its way into her stories as her characters often find themselves in beautiful natural settings. When she isn't writing, Gerri and her longtime partner, Diane, keep busy at their log cabin in East Texas tending to their two vegetable gardens, orchard and five acres of piney woods. They share their lives with two Australian shepherds and an assortment of furry felines.

CHAPTER ONE

Jordan Sims drove slowly, her gaze drawn again and again to the bay, its bluish green water shimmering in the bright morning sunlight. She should have come out here earlier in the week, but she wanted to at least wait until the funeral…wait until her brother was laid to rest before invading his beach house.

Oh, sure, it was still her parents' old weekend place, and her grandparents' house before that. But Matt had made the small house on the bay his own once her parents had stopped spending time there. Of course, she hadn't been around then. She'd already left home, escaping to college and then to Chicago.

And she hadn't been back. Not really. In the last fifteen years, she could count on one hand the number of times she'd been back to Rockport. A few days at Christmas, mostly. And once, her mother had talked her into a week over Thanksgiving. God, that had been endless.

Yet here she was, taking a leave of absence from her job, intending to stay on the Texas coast "as long as you need me," as she'd told her parents. The restaurant, they could handle. Matt didn't have a hand in it. But the store? No, that was Matt's baby. He'd turned their little souvenir shop into a thriving business. All because of Fat Larry.

She shook her head but smiled nonetheless. The pudgy pelican had become a fixture in Rockport. Everyone knew Fat Larry. In fact, if you asked directions along Austin Street, Fat Larry was the landmark the locals used.

"Go two blocks past Fat Larry. Can't miss it."

"If you get to Fat Larry, you've gone too far."

Fat Larry was a ten-foot-tall plastic pelican—purple, no less—with a bright green T-shirt advertising the store—Sims' Treasures. Of course, all the locals referred to the store as Fat Larry's. Her brother, with not a single hour of college credit to his name, had a knack for marketing. And it all started with Fat Larry. The shop was *the* go-to place for Rockport and Texas Gulf Coast souvenirs. Matt liked to have fun and he was a natural in the store with customers. On any given day, he'd start tossing Fat Larry T-shirts out. They cost next to nothing to produce and offered legions of free advertising.

But a single-car accident on a stormy April night had taken her brother's life, leaving the store—and Fat Larry—in a state of disarray. Since his death, the store had been left to run on its own, with the part-time employees filling in where they could. Matt didn't have full-time workers any longer, not since Marge Nguyen had married and moved to Corpus. Her father had gone there a couple of times to make sure they weren't "stealing us blind." But they had the restaurant to run. They couldn't— and didn't have the drive to—run the store too.

"So, Jordan, let's quit our job and close up the condo," she murmured.

To say she'd had second—and third, fourth and fifth— thoughts about her decision would be an understatement. Who quit a six-figure job to come back home to run a souvenir shop?

Not quit, she reminded herself. Leave of absence. Two or three months…four at the most, she'd told her boss. She'd have her laptop. If something came up that her assistant couldn't handle, she could take care of it remotely. Because with Matt gone, her parents had no one to turn to. They could always sell the store, but as her father had said, it brought in as much money as the restaurant did. It would be crazy to sell it. Her father was at least thinking of the future. Her mother, not so much. She was still in a state of shock over Matt's sudden death. Jordan couldn't blame her. Matt was her baby, Matt was the one who stayed at home, Matt was the one who went into the family business.

She pushed her thoughts away, knowing it was her choice to leave home, her choice to stay away as much as she did. It was her choice to make a new life in the big city, far, far away from the small coastal town of Rockport, Texas.

She turned onto Bayside, the street that would take her to the little one-lane road called Pelican Drive. Oak trees would swallow up the view of Copano Bay, she knew, so she kept her gaze on the water as long as she could. She slowed, then turned to the right, surprised at how familiar the road was to her. It had been six years since she'd been out here. Most of the lots were bigger, the houses older, than the ones nearer Rockport on Aransas Bay to the south. When she was a kid, she was jealous of those living there, with their fancy boats that could be in the Gulf in a matter of minutes. But by the time she was in high school, she was thankful their little beach house was hidden back here in the oaks. No tourists, no traffic and no close neighbors. It was like they had the bay to themselves on those long summer days.

She slowed again as the road ended in a large cul-de-sac lined with ancient oaks. She looked up to where the old sign that her grandfather had chiseled out many, many years ago still hung. *Pelican's Landing*, the name her grandmother had given the beach house when they'd first built it. The sign was badly in need of a paint job and she noticed that the chain had come loose on one side, causing it to hang crooked. But what was perched on top of the sign made her laugh. A mini version of Fat Larry, T-shirt and all, pointed down the narrow driveway. She was still smiling as she took the twisting drive that skirted the large trees, and she noted that for as much as Matt loved the beach house, yard work obviously wasn't high on his priority list. The shrubs needed trimming and the grass needed to be mowed. The bougainvillea at the edge of the carport was blooming nicely though.

She pulled into the empty carport and shut off the engine of her rental car. She paused only a moment before getting out. Again, a sense that she was invading Matt's space hit her and she shook it away. If she was going to stay in Rockport for the next few months, she would stay out here, not with her parents. She was used to living alone and so were they.

But instead of going inside the house, she was drawn to the bay. She took the sidewalk down to the pier. It looked neglected as well and she took a tentative step on it, feeling it shift beneath her. She walked out on it anyway, her gaze traveling across the water, the gentle waves slapping the pier as the breeze and high tide rolled the bay. It was a pleasant spring day, the sky nearly cloudless. Of course, she was back in Texas. May was sometimes considered more summer than spring. Even early May, like today.

She took a deep breath, the smell of the salty air bringing back memories of her childhood. She remembered running down this very pier, her bare feet pounding on the boards as she took flight at the end, splashing into the water with the carefree attitude that only a child can possess. She was four years older than Matt, but he tried to keep up with her. She taught him to swim right here in the bay too. As they got older, Jet Skis replaced swimming and they would race out into the open water where the causeway crossed over, dodging shrimp boats and fishermen alike.

She smiled as she remembered all the fun they'd had. But by the time she was a junior in high school, things changed. *She* changed. Because she had a secret she dared not tell a soul, not even her brother.

She was gay. And scared to death.

So she slowly withdrew from Matt, from her parents. She focused solely on her schoolwork, vowing to graduate with honors and secure enough scholarships to take her away from

Rockport and go to where no one knew her. Where no one would judge her if her secret got out. By the time she was a senior, only a few friends remained. Matt was not one of them.

She went to California, thinking she would be safe there. And she was. College was fun and she met many like-minded people. She no longer had to keep her secret to herself. Yet she hadn't counted on her parents finding out, on Matt finding out. When they did, she withdrew even more. She couldn't stand seeing her mother's tears. It took her nearly fifteen years to realize they still loved her, that they'd always loved her.

But by then, she was entrenched in her job, her long hours at work having paid off. She'd moved up to the executive level, her salary finally equaling her stress level. Well...almost.

She sighed and turned around, heading back toward the house. Oh, she loved her job. She really did. It was fast-paced and never dull. While she no longer worked seventy-hour weeks, she still put in at least sixty hours. That, of course, left little time for a personal life. No doubt that was why it had been so easy to leave there. There was no one who would miss her.

She walked up the stairs to the deck, pausing to glance back at the water once more before fishing the key from her pocket. Matt's key. She squeezed it tightly in her hand for a guilty second, then unlocked the door.

She stared at the mess in a moment of shock. If she didn't know how lacking Matt's housekeeping skills were, she would have thought the place had been ransacked. She absently picked up the newspapers lying around and piled them up on the coffee table. Flip-flops were on the floor beside the sofa and a towel was on the back of the recliner. She shook her head as she picked up the towel, taking it with her.

She took one look into the kitchen and quickly turned away. God only knew how long the dirty dishes had been piled up in the sink. Thoughts of cleaning the house on her own vanished. She would definitely hire a cleaning crew. And perhaps a yard crew too.

She made her way into the master bedroom. Jeans were tossed on the floor and she picked them up too, folding them neatly before placing them on the unmade bed. She didn't bother going into his bathroom. She could envision the mess without having to see it. Instead, she went to the double doors that opened up onto the side deck shaded by a large oak tree. She went to the railing, glancing once at the neighbor's place, then turning her attention to the bay. Memories streamed through her mind, some flashing quickly, others lingering. This was her grandparents' little piece of heaven, and she and Matt had spent many a lazy summer day here…making memories.

She heard a car door slam and, with a sigh, went back inside. "Jordan?"

"Back here, Mom," she called.

She gave her mother a gentle smile when she paused at the bedroom door, noting the sadness in her eyes. She wondered how long it would take before she saw laughter there again.

"I haven't been here in so long, I had no idea the extent of the mess," her mother apologized. "But you know how Matt is." She swallowed. "Was," she corrected.

"Yes, I know," Jordan said. "And I'm not going to attempt to clean it myself."

"Of course not. I'll get Maria to come out here," she said, referring to the woman who cleaned her own house on a weekly basis. Her mother turned a circle in the room. "What should we do with his things?"

"Mom," she said, going to her. "Let me do this. You don't have to."

Her mother shook her head. "You always assume your children will outlive you. This isn't something you can prepare for."

"I know." She spread her arms out. "We'll give his clothes away to a…a charity or a church or something," she said.

"It doesn't look like he's got too many personal things here. More at his office, I think. And he's still got things at the house too." Her mother blinked tears away. "I can't throw his things out like they mean nothing to us."

"We've got time, Mom. It's only been two days since the funeral. Nothing says we have to rush through it."

Her mother nodded sharply. "Yes. We can take our time. Because I can't deal with it right now. Not this soon." She glanced at her watch. "I need to get to the restaurant. Your father will need help with the lunch crowd and I need to…get back into the swing of things." She looked at Jordan. "And Fat Larry…what are we going to do about that? Matt—"

"I told you, I'll handle it. I've got a degree in finance, Mom. I think I can manage," she said. "I'll go by first thing in the morning."

"One of the girls who work for him…Annie Thomas…she's the one who's been running things. She's been there a couple of years now."

"Do you have her phone number?"

"Well, I know her parents, of course, but no, I don't have her number. She and Matt went to high school together. They were close, I think."

Jordan nodded, wondering if they'd been dating. "Okay, I'll find her," she said. She went to her mother and hugged her tight. "Don't worry about Fat Larry. And don't worry about all this," she said, motioning to the room. "I'll take care of it."

Her mother gave her a smile which didn't reach her eyes. "Thank you for being here, Jordan. It means so much to me. To us."

"Like I said, I'll be here as long as you need me."

She let out a heavy sigh as her mother left, then she turned back to the room, mindlessly stripping the bed as she tried to formulate a plan to get the house cleaned.

CHAPTER TWO

"What do you think they're going to do about the store?" Suzanne asked.

Annie shrugged her shoulders. "Don't know," she said.

It was the same question and answer they'd had between them several times during the last ten days. They were headed to Fat Larry's now, walking slowly down the sidewalk. Annie always parked at the marina near the city park and walked to the store. It was her lone form of exercise these days.

"I still can't believe Matt's gone."

"I know. How do you think I feel? I was the last one to see him alive."

And of course she knew what Suzanne's next statement would be.

"I still can't believe you *slept* with him," Suzanne nearly whispered. "And then he dies the same night."

Annie sighed. "I know."

"So did you, you know, like him?"

Annie rolled her eyes. They weren't in high school any longer, yet sometimes Suzanne acted like they'd never left.

"I liked him fine. He was cute. He was fun."

"But I mean, did you—"

"No, Suzanne. Not like that. In fact, it was pretty much a disaster," she admitted. She stopped walking, turning to Suzanne. "I only slept with him…well, because I haven't been with anyone since Derrick." She impatiently tucked a strand of blond hair behind her ear. "I was starting to think something was wrong with me."

"Oh, my God! Are you serious? You've been divorced four years." Suzanne grabbed her arm and pulled her closer. "What about that guy from Corpus?"

"Jason? I never slept with him," she said.

Suzanne dropped her arm and they continued walking. "What do you mean, something was wrong with you?"

Annie shrugged again, not sure how to explain to Suzanne how she felt. While she and Suzanne were close, good friends in fact, she still didn't confide too much in her. Suzanne was still married to Derrick's best friend.

"I haven't had any interest in sex," she finally admitted. She didn't add that that was one of the major issues between her and Derrick. She had no desire to sleep with him. "The night I was with Matt, I didn't either. I was going through the motions, nothing more. And then I started crying afterward and he freaked out." She paused. "I mean, he was my boss. We're in his office on the sofa. And we're naked and I'm crying and he's apologizing and through it all, I'm thinking, 'Great, now I've got to get a new job.' The thought of facing him every day, well, I knew I couldn't do it."

"Oh, my God," Suzanne said again. "And then he died. You must have felt awful."

"Yeah, thanks for reminding me," she said as she pulled out her keys. But she stopped short when she opened the front door to Fat Larry's, shocked to see someone inside. The woman was behind the counter, snooping around. For a moment, Annie panicked. Were they getting robbed? Then the woman looked up, a smile on her face. She looked friendly—and familiar—so Annie relaxed. "Can I help you?" she asked.

The woman came around the counter, her hand extended. "I'm Jordan Sims."

Annie stared at her blankly before the name registered. "You're Matt's sister." Of course she was. She'd seen her at the funeral. Besides, the resemblance was uncanny. Dark hair, dark eyes. Tall and lean, much as Matt had been. Jordan was dressed in an expensive-looking business suit, and Annie felt a little out of place in her shorts. Nonetheless, she reached for her hand, shaking a quick greeting.

"Yes. Older sister."

"I've...Matt's mentioned you before," she said vaguely, wondering why she was suddenly nervous. "I'm Annie Thomas." She motioned beside her to where Suzanne had been standing by mutely. "This is my friend, Suzanne. She...she doesn't work here. She came by with me to open up." Annie looked around. "Or...is that what you're going to do?"

"No, no. I was actually hoping you'd show up. My mother said you had been handling things since...well, since Matt's accident."

"Yes. And I'm so sorry," she said automatically.

"Thank you." Jordan turned away, heading back to the counter, before pausing. "Nice to meet you, Suzanne."

Suzanne nodded. "You too." She then leaned closer to Annie. "My cue to leave, I guess."

"I'll call you later," she said quietly, her gaze on Jordan and not Suzanne. What was she doing here? she wondered. Was she taking over? Well, there was only one way to find out. She walked closer to the counter, glancing around to see if anything was out of order. It appeared to be as she'd left it yesterday evening.

"I didn't mean to run your friend off," Jordan said.

Annie waved away her apology. "Suzanne doesn't work so she's got a lot of free time." Jordan raised her eyebrows expectantly and Annie went on to explain. "Her husband works on oil rigs—offshore. Ten days on, ten days off. And her daughter is in the third grade."

"I see. Must be nice not to have to work," Jordan said as she leaned casually against the counter.

Annie smiled slightly, not wanting to contradict her. But when she'd been married to Derrick, she'd been a housewife like Suzanne. And she had hated it. She often wondered if they'd had a child, would she still be married?

"So…are you going to take over the store?" she asked.

"For the time being, yes," Jordan said. "I used to work in here some when I was in high school." Jordan looked at her pointedly. "Did we know each other then?"

At that, Annie laughed. "I guess not, if you don't remember me."

Jordan nodded. "I don't get back much. I never really kept in touch with anyone."

"I was in Matt's grade," she explained as she walked around the counter and put her purse on the shelf. "I think you were a senior when we were just lowly freshmen."

"I see. Well, by the time I was a senior—" But Jordan didn't finish her sentence. Instead she paused, looking around the store. "So, the sign says we open at nine. Most of the other stores open at ten." She looked at her watch. "Yet you're here at eight."

Annie nodded. "The first hour is spent getting ready. Refolding T-shirts, mainly, and getting things back in order," she said, going to one of the displays against the wall and holding up a shirt. "Customers pick them up, look at them, then toss them on top." She automatically folded the shirt without thinking. It was a chore she'd been doing for the last two years. Then she, too, looked at her watch. She wasn't surprised that Jessica was late again. She was always late. But ever since…well, ever since Matt's been gone, Jessica had been coming in later than usual.

"I'll help you do that if you'll first give me a quick rundown on the place," Jordan said.

"Actually, Jessica is supposed to be here," she said as she placed the shirt in the proper bin. She headed toward the door marked Private. "First thing, coffee."

Jordan followed her and Annie watched as Jordan did a quick inspection, her gaze traveling across the room, landing on another door.

"That's…his office," Annie said quietly. She felt a lump in her throat as memories of that last night with Matt surfaced.

She shook them away, instead going to the coffeepot and filling it with water.

"My mother says she thought Matt stayed here quite a bit."

"There's a sofa in there," she said. "He spent a lot of nights here. During the summer, we are so busy, it was easier for him to be here." She glanced at Jordan quickly. "There are still three weeks—four in some places—until the public schools let out, but things were already picking up. Birders," she said.

"Birders?"

"Spring migration."

Jordan nodded. "Oh. Bird watchers. Do you cater to them?"

"Yes. We have a whole shelf of environmental T-shirts and some funny birding shirts. Then the ironwood carvings of birds. Those are a big hit." She added coffee grounds to the basket, then turned the coffeemaker on.

"I noticed a…a popcorn thing out there."

Annie smiled. "Matt said the smell of freshly popped corn would bring people in off the street. And it did. We keep a bin of cold bottled water too. We make the first batch of popcorn about eleven," she explained. "All free."

They both turned when the door opened and a yawning Jessica came in with a mumbled "Good morning."

"You're late," Annie said. "Again."

Jessica shrugged. "Does it matter? Matt never cared if I was late."

Annie looked at Jordan and smiled. Jordan raised her eyebrows.

"Do we have…like, timecards or something?"

"No. Matt believed in the honor system," she said.

"Who's she?" Jessica asked as she waited patiently beside the coffeepot as it dripped. "Did you hire someone?"

"Not exactly," Annie said.

Jordan stepped forward and held out her hand. "I'm Jordan. Your new boss."

Jessica at least had the good sense to look embarrassed. "New boss?"

"Yes. I'm Matt's sister. And unlike him, I don't believe in the honor system." Jordan turned to Annie. "Who else is supposed to work today?"

Annie pointed to the whiteboard. "We keep the schedule up here. Staci comes in at noon, leaves at six. Jessica is here until one. This is Brandon's long day. He comes at one and works until closing," she said.

"So only two of you here at one time? Is that enough?"

"Well, Matt was always here too. And in the summer, he would hire a couple of high school kids to work." The coffee had finished brewing and as soon as Jessica poured a cup, Annie did the same. "Would you like some?" she offered Jordan.

"No, thanks. I was up at five and drank a whole pot already."

"Five? Who gets up at five?" Jessica asked as she took a sip.

"People who have work to do," Jordan said pointedly.

Jessica nodded. "I should probably...you know, start on the T-shirts."

Annie smiled quickly. "Good idea."

As soon as she was out the door, Annie turned to Jordan. "She's a liability."

"But she's cute," Jordan said. "I'm sure that was why Matt hired her."

Annie laughed. "You knew him well, I see."

"Is that why you got hired?"

Annie felt a blush light her face. "No. I had to beg for the job," she said honestly. "Matt likes to hire, well, younger people."

"You're what? Thirty?"

Annie shook her head. "Don't rush me. I'm still clinging to twenty-nine," she said. "Jessica, for instance, is nineteen. Brandon is twenty-three, but he's worked here since he was in high school. Staci is twenty-one."

Jordan stared at the schedule on the whiteboard. "So if Staci comes at noon but Jessica doesn't leave until one, then you'll have an hour free?"

"What do you mean?"

"I've got a ton of questions. I'd like to sit down with you and go over everything. Noon?" Jordan turned to her. "What is your schedule?"

"Well, this is the week before finals. Dead week, they call it. I've been able to be here every day. I'm the only one who knows how to close. But next week—"

"Finals?"

"College," she said.

"Oh. I assumed—"

"I'm a late bloomer," she explained. She didn't add that it was her divorce that prompted her to go back to college.

"Okay. So today you're here, but not next week?"

"And this weekend, if you need me."

"Let's go over all of that at lunch then," Jordan said.

"That's fine." She pointed to the door. "I should go help Jessica. We'll be opening soon."

Jordan nodded. "Thanks, Annie. For taking care of things since...well, since the accident. My family...we appreciate that."

Annie topped off her coffee cup. "It's no problem. Matt was a friend," she said.

She left Jordan Sims then, going out into the store where Jessica had the music already playing. Matt had insisted on oldies. Anything from the sixties or seventies. She had to admit, the music had grown on her as she hummed along with an old Beach Boys tune.

She went about the routine of straightening the items on the display shelves—mostly knickknacks depicting life on the beach. They had the customary bins of seashells, but Matt had also added rocks. Quartz and crystals, agates and geodes, and even fossils now had a prominent display along one wall. She looked around. It wasn't your typical souvenir shop. It had a nice variety of items, not only T-shirts and coffee mugs. Matt always said he wanted to keep it diverse with a good vibe. To him, summer beach music and fresh popcorn took care of the vibe.

As if on cue, a Jimmy Buffett song came on. One of Matt's favorites, she noted. She suddenly missed him very much.

CHAPTER THREE

Jordan didn't know Annie's preference but thought she couldn't go wrong with a turkey sandwich from Subway. She picked up two and headed back to the store. She'd spent the morning going through Matt's bedroom at the beach house. She'd thought it would be a hard, emotional task, but there were very few personal things there. Not a single picture was to be found and the walls were bare, except for a poster showing a surfer riding a wave. Yesterday, she'd gone about the task of stacking dirty clothes in one pile and clean in another. Mostly shorts, jeans, T-shirts. She'd dropped the clean clothes off at the local Goodwill store this morning. The dirty clothes were in a bag near the washer. She'd stripped the sheets and had washed them yesterday. At two this afternoon, Maria was going to meet her out there to start cleaning. She hoped she could sleep there tonight instead of at her parents' house.

Earlier at the store, she'd only peeked inside his office. It was in a state of disarray and she couldn't believe he actually functioned that way. She was quite the opposite. She couldn't stand clutter of any kind on her desk. But until she knew more about how the store operated, she would leave it as she found it.

She went in through the back door instead of the front and headed directly into the cluttered office. She placed the sandwiches and chips on the desk, then went back out to the small kitchen. The fridge was stocked with water bottles and beer—Matt's favorite brew—nothing else. She shook her head as she pulled out two waters.

"Oh, you're back."

She turned, smiling as Annie stood in the doorway watching her. "Just got here. I brought lunch. I didn't know what your normal routine is."

"Popcorn," she said, holding up a small bag.

"I got us Subway. Turkey sandwiches," she said.

"Sounds better than popcorn," Annie said as she tossed a few in her mouth. "But it is addicting."

Jordan motioned to the office. "Eat in there?"

"Okay. I guess you'll want to go over his setup."

"The office is a mess. Is there a setup?"

Annie laughed. "Matt couldn't work with a clean desk. He swore he knew where everything was."

Jordan sat at his desk and shoved some papers out of the way. Annie took a visitor's chair and she, too, moved papers to the side.

"What is all this?"

"Even though everything is on the computer, Matt still liked to print it out. Shipping receipts, inventory, orders," she said with a wave of her hand.

"What did he use for his accounting system? QuickBooks?"

"Yes. That's where we keep our timesheets too," Annie said, motioning to the laptop.

"So that's Matt's honor system? You log in and post your time?" she asked as she took a bite of the sandwich.

"Not exactly. Matt logged in every morning. We only put our time in. Well, we're supposed to. If someone forgets, he would use the whiteboard and put in the hours based on the schedule."

Jordan's eyes widened. "So everyone would have access to the whole accounting system?"

Annie nodded. "Yes."

"Amazing." She shook her head. "Maybe I've worked at the corporate level too long."

"Where do you live?"

"Chicago," she said. "I work in the financial sector."

Annie smiled as she bit into her sandwich. "And this whole setup is just *wrong*?" she teased.

"On so many levels," Jordan stated. She wiped her mouth. "So he used QuickBooks for accounting and payroll. Did he outsource anything?"

"No. We did all of it in-house."

"How familiar are you with his operation?"

"I've helped him with pretty much everything except ordering. Other than Matt, I'm the only one who knows how to close. I pay the bills and normally do payroll. He handled all of the ordering," Annie said.

"So you're authorized to sign checks?"

"No. He signs a bunch in advance. But most of the payables are done online."

Jordan shook her head. "And the checkbook was kept locked in a safe somewhere?" she asked hopefully.

Annie laughed. "No. It's in the top drawer of his desk. And we'll need to do payroll today. Friday is payday, but I didn't feel comfortable doing it without authorization. Every other Friday is payday. Besides, I assume you'll need to make arrangements with the bank to sign checks now."

"Yes, I'm heading to the bank as soon as I leave here." Jordan studied her for a moment, then asked the one question that had been nagging at her all morning. "Why do you work here?"

"Excuse me?"

Jordan took a sip from her water. "You said you were in college. A late bloomer."

"Yes, I did."

"So?"

"So even though I'm not a traditional college student, I still need a job."

Jordan glanced at her hands. "Not married?"

Annie met her gaze. "Is that relevant?"

"Of course not. I'm just curious. You've been running the store. I have to trust you. I wanted to know more about you."

"Oh." Annie set her sandwich down and reached for her water bottle too, perhaps stalling for time. "Well, yeah. I was married. Right out of high school. That's why I didn't go to college."

"Why couldn't you still go to college?"

"Because...because I was stupid," Annie said with a sigh. "There were three of us. Suzanne and Macy and me. We married guys from high school. All friends. All a year ahead of us. The guys had jobs already. Oil. Offshore. And they all had this idea of the perfect little housewife and soon-to-be mother of their children. They didn't want us to work. And at the time, I was content to stay at home and get the house fixed up." She shook her head. "Like I said, stupid. But his parents had money, they bought us a house and I just fell into this...this trap."

"Kids?"

"God, no. I would probably still be married." She picked a piece of turkey from her sandwich and nibbled it. "There was a lot of drama. Derrick didn't want me doing anything. When he was home, he wanted me there. For ten days. Then he'd go back to the rig for ten days and I'd be stuck there. Macy got pregnant right away. Suzanne shortly after that." Annie met her gaze. "Even though I'd told him I did, I never got off the pill."

Jordan smiled. "Surely he suspected."

"Derrick is not smart enough," Annie said quickly. "Anyway, I told him I had to *do* something. I couldn't sit at home anymore. I felt stagnant. So I got a job at the elementary school as a teacher's aide. And I loved it."

"And he hated it?"

"Yes. And we constantly fought and argued. I'd had enough. I filed for divorce while he was offshore. Moved back in with my parents at the age of twenty-five."

"And then what?"

"Why am I telling you all this? You are a complete stranger to me," Annie said.

Jordan shrugged. "I look like Matt."

Annie nodded. "Yes, you do. But he was never this serious."

"Serious?"

"Very short attention span."

Jordan laughed. "Yeah, that never changed." Her smile faded. "Were you two…close?"

"Close? Well, high school. And I've been here two years or so," Annie said.

Jordan noticed a blush on her face. "Dated?"

Annie met her gaze. "Not really, no."

"Not really? Or no?"

Annie picked up her sandwich again. "No."

"Okay. So you divorced. Then what?"

"After the drama died down, I started college. Texas A&M in Corpus. I still worked as a teacher's aide about fifteen hours a week. But it didn't pay much at all. I knew Matt was looking for part-time help, so I came by here. And yes, I really did have to beg for the job."

"So how much school do you have left?"

Annie smiled. "I'm almost through. Finals next week, then I'm off for the summer. I have a light load in the fall, then I do my student teaching next spring."

"And where will you teach?"

"Here in Rockport. I've got a great relationship with the principal, Mr. Early. One of the elementary teachers is retiring next year. I'll do my student teaching under her, then I'll take over her class the next year."

"So Fat Larry will lose you soon?"

Annie laughed. "I'm afraid so."

"But you're off all summer from school. Does that mean you could work here full time?"

"Full-time? Oh, that would be great."

"Good. Because Fat Larry needs an office manager."

"Office manager? Really? Then what will you do?" Annie asked innocently.

Jordan laughed. "Supervise, of course."

CHAPTER FOUR

Jordan walked through the busy restaurant and into the kitchen, the smell of fried seafood bringing back delicious memories. Her father was dressed in his whites, chef's hat and all, as he battered fish. Her mother ran the ordering system, juggling in-house orders with those placed online. She still couldn't believe Matt had talked them into that but apparently it was working.

"Busy tonight, huh?" she said as she gave her mother a quick kiss on the cheek.

"Yes, Friday nights are always like this." She eyed her. "You had a busy day yourself?"

"Yeah. Got to visit with Annie Thomas. She's nice. I'm going to hire her full time for the summer."

"You are? But—"

"Let me run the store, Mom. You have your hands full here."

"I know, I know," she said. "Are you hungry? Did you come for dinner?"

Jordan smiled. "I placed an order online."

Her mother's eyes widened. "You did?"

Jordan pulled her phone out of her pocket, looking at the time. "Supposed to be ready in ten minutes."

Her mother nodded. "So? Maria went by Pelican's Landing?"

"Yes. She had another woman with her. It only took them three hours to clean the place. You won't recognize it," she said.

"And Matt's things?"

"I've got everything boxed up," she said. "There wasn't that much there. And I've already taken his clothes." She saw the sadness in her mother's eyes. "Keeping his clothes, Mom, didn't make sense."

"I thought we would wait—"

"Not for the clothes," she said. "Someone will get use out of them."

"I know you're right, Jordan. But giving away his things, well, it—"

"Makes it final?" she guessed.

Her mother nodded. "And makes it real."

"I know," she said gently. "I'm sorry."

"We should have taken more time," her mother said. "But your father, well, being here at the restaurant makes everything seem…somewhat normal."

"And that's what you need," she said. "Matt wouldn't want you sitting at home grieving, you know that."

"Well, being here keeps my mind occupied, at least."

"Yes. Now, I'm starving." She looked around, seeing a take-out box being stuffed with fish and shrimp. "I think that's mine."

Her mother bagged it for her, then added two tubs of tartar sauce. Jordan smiled, glad her mother remembered that she loved the stuff. She also noted that she omitted the cabbage slaw, something Jordan hated.

"So you're staying there tonight? Not at the house?"

"Yeah, I'm going to stay there. I already have my things in the car." She met her mother's gaze. "That's okay, isn't it?"

"Of course. We liked having you at the house, though."

"Yes, it was nice. But…you know, I'm used to being alone."

"I know you are. Will we still see you every day? Do you need some help with the store?"

"It's under control. Annie's going to keep it running pretty much like Matt did. There are only a couple of things I'm going to change," she said. "And yes, you'll still see me every day."

Her mother's eyes sharpened. "What are you changing? Matt knew—"

"Nothing major, Mom. Logging in timesheets, mainly. Matt was very lax. They're paid hourly. I'm going to install a punch clock," she said.

"That's kinda old-fashioned, isn't it?"

Jordan laughed. "It's sort of a virtual one. It's on the computer. It's an add-on to QuickBooks. It'll make payroll easier too."

"Do you know how to do all of that?"

"Yes. Now don't worry about the store." She took the bag, already imagining biting into her father's famous battered fish. "Let me get out of your hair. You're too busy to be chatting." She kissed her mother's cheek again, then snuck around the fry station to do the same to her father. "Dad, thanks for dinner."

"I made the fish extra spicy, like you like it."

"Great. I'm sure it'll be perfect. See you later."

Of course, she didn't make it back to Pelican's Landing before sneaking a nibble of the fish. As promised, spicy. There were five fillets and at least a dozen jumbo shrimp. She would have enough left over for lunch tomorrow. At least she hoped so as she ate her third shrimp.

The beach house seemed almost empty with all of Matt's clutter—mess—gone. A lot of the things left in the house were from her grandparents. Like the collection of conch shells which, as a child, she used to love to play with. These weren't bought in a treasure shop, though. No, these were all found on the beach. Her grandmother had been a beachcomber. Not that you could find much here along the bay. Her grandmother, twice a week, would drive to the ferry and go across to Port Aransas, hitting the beach before sunrise.

On her way to the kitchen, she paused to glance at the shelf that held small baskets of sand dollars and smaller shells. She'd been with her grandmother when they'd found a lot of those. She'd always been close to her. That was yet another regret she had. By staying away, she missed out on her grandmother's last years. Years she could never get back. Same with Matt. The years passed them by so rapidly, she hardly noticed. With a sigh, she pushed the guilt away.

Matt had a nice collection of wine, all red. She chose a bottle and opened it, then poured a generous amount into a glass. She took that, along with her food, out to the deck. The sun had set, but there was still a little color left in the sky. The early evening breeze was pleasant, and she didn't bother with the ceiling fan. She opened up her box and grabbed a piece of fish with her fingers, plunging it into the tub of tartar sauce.

"So good," she murmured around the bite.

She leaned back, sipping from her wine. This, she was used to. Being alone, having dinner alone. The view from her condo couldn't compete with this, however. Pink and red still shimmered on the water, and she watched as a fishing boat cruised out in the bay, heading back to the marina in Fulton or maybe Rockport. A quiet peacefulness settled over her, and she wondered how long she'd be content to stay here, so far away from the big city rush that was her life. Could she endure three, four months of this? Would her job wait for her? Peter had told her to take as much time as she needed. Her position in the company afforded her that, at least. She hadn't worked her ass off for nothing. But still, she had responsibilities there. Of course, she had responsibilities here too, she reminded herself. She'd neglected her family for far too many years. Her parents needed her now and she intended to honor that obligation.

She dunked another shrimp into the tartar sauce, enjoying the crunch of her father's secret batter. She wondered if her mother even knew the recipe he used. As darkness settled over the bay, the fish and shrimp she'd intended to save for lunch tomorrow were dwindling fast, as was the wine. One fillet and two shrimp remained. She pushed the box away and emptied the rest of the wine into her glass.

Full darkness now and the breeze off the bay was actually cool. She let her thoughts drift to Fat Larry. Matt had turned the store into a success and she didn't think she was going to change anything. Well, other than the time-keeping. Matt may have been content to pay them based on what they were *supposed* to work, but she was not. Tomorrow she would attack his office and try to spend some time with the books. And inventory. Maybe Annie would be able to help with that.

Annie had been in Matt's grade in school, yet she had no recollection of her. She looked younger than the twenty-nine she claimed to be. Blond hair and blue-green eyes, she was certainly attractive. Matt was a fool if he hadn't tried to date her.

Oh well. Right now, all she cared about was Annie helping her run the store. Maybe by the end of summer, when Annie went back to college and Jordan could escape back to Chicago, she'd have hired someone to manage it for them. That is, if her father would trust an outsider to run the business. Because even though the store had Matt's stamp all over it, her father had started it many, many years ago, even before they'd opened the restaurant. At the time, it was simply a little store that sold nothing more than trinkets and shells and a handful of T-shirts. Once they'd opened the restaurant, they'd almost neglected the store. But Matt had taken it over and made it what it was today…a landmark in Rockport. And tourists came to the store to buy a memento or two of their vacation—and to take a picture with Fat Larry, the pudgy, purple pelican.

CHAPTER FIVE

Annie was ten minutes early, yet Jordan had beaten her again to the store. She found the coffee already made and heard her rustling in Matt's office. Well, Jordan's office now, she supposed. She still wasn't certain what to make of Jordan Sims. In looks, she certainly favored Matt, although she was not nearly as tall as Matt had been. But dark hair, dark eyes, an easy smile—they were alike in that regard. She suspected Jordan's personality was a little more on the serious side, a little more purposeful than Matt had been. Matt liked to have fun and never wanted to cause waves. His employees loved him because he didn't have a lot of rules. She guessed that was about to change.

She poured a cup of coffee, then stuck her head in the office. It hardly looked like the same place. She eyed the trash bag, seeing it stuffed with papers. Jordan was busy delving into one of Matt's drawers. Annie noted that again, Jordan was dressed in pressed slacks and a crisp blouse. She looked down at her own bare legs and flip-flops. The only time she wore jeans or slacks were during the few really cold days in January or February.

"Good morning," she said as she took a sip of coffee.

Jordan looked up from her task, smiling as she saw Annie. "Hey. Is it eight already?"

"Just about." She stared at the trash, then raised an eyebrow. "Couldn't stand the clutter?"

"Not a second longer," Jordan said. "Besides, I took a look at his books. All of this," she said, motioning to the papers in the trash bag, "is documented, at your fingertips with a click of the mouse."

"Yes, he was a bit old school when it came to paper copies," she said. "Can I get you some coffee?"

Jordan nodded. "Thanks. I made it but completely forgot about it."

"How do you take it?"

"Black," Jordan said as she pulled out another pile of papers from a drawer. "And thanks for doing payroll yesterday."

"No problem."

Annie filled a mug with coffee and brought it back, setting it carefully on the edge of the desk before sitting down across from it. "Did you get the punch clock add-on you were telling me about?"

"Yes. It's already loaded to QuickBooks. I'll show you how to use it, then you can teach everyone else." Jordan sipped from her coffee. "I also ordered another laptop for them to use. We'll keep it out there," she said.

"Don't want them in here?" Annie guessed.

Jordan smiled but didn't answer. Instead, she asked, "Are Saturdays the busiest days?"

"Usually," Annie said. "But once school is out and the tourists come, then every day is about the same."

"And we're only open on Sundays during the summer?"

"There's not a set start date," she said. "Whenever things begin picking up, like the spring migration, then we start opening on Sundays. Right now, it's only noon until five."

"So who works it?"

Annie smiled. "Matt always did. So I guess you."

Jordan's eyes widened. "Alone? You'd leave me here alone?"

Annie laughed. "Well, you *are* the boss."

"Yeah. Back here," Jordan said, pointing to the laptop. "In the office, with the finances and stuff. Not out there with, you know, people."

Annie thought Jordan was surely teasing but the look in her eyes said the fright was genuine. "So you and Matt...just the opposite, huh?"

"What do you mean?"

"Matt loved being out with the customers. He hated office work," she said. "Which is why he taught me a lot of it."

Jordan nodded. "My experience with working with customers is over the phone or email. I rarely meet our clients in person."

"What is it that you do?"

"The company I'm with...well, we're diverse. Financial sector, like I said. We do investing, acquisitions. Buy small companies and then either sell them or merge them. We have clients all over the world."

"Wall Street stuff?"

"That too. But we're based in Chicago."

"So our little operation here is—"

"Scary. It involves real people."

"And yours doesn't?"

"No, not really. It's...well, it's only numbers."

The outer door to the store opened and Annie turned in her seat, seeing Jessica sneaking in. Before she could say anything, Jordan got up and walked out to her.

"You're fifteen minutes late," Jordan said. "Do you not like working here or what?"

Jessica's eyes widened. "Yes. Yes, I do."

"So you want to change your hours then? Instead of eight, you want to make it eight thirty?"

Annie very nearly felt sorry for Jessica. The girl apparently didn't have a clue as to what Jordan was trying to say to her. Jessica looked past Jordan to her, but Annie simply stared at her.

"I guess...I guess I could come in at eight thirty," she finally said.

"Good," Jordan said. "I'll change the schedule then. And if you're late again…you're fired."

"But…Matt—"

"Matt is not here. I am."

Jordan turned and headed back to the office, and Annie noticed that she had to hide a smile. It was a cushy job and they all knew it. Besides, Matt was paying them all a dollar more an hour than any of the other shops in town paid. She suspected Jessica would be early from now on.

"So…where were we?"

Annie smiled at her. "You were saying you were scared of people."

"Oh, yeah. So does that mean you'll work on Sunday?"

Annie nodded. "I can work on Sunday. But remember, I won't be here all next week. I need to show you how to close and reconcile."

"Right. And you'll start full time the following week?"

"Yes. I'm actually looking forward to it."

"Great. Then we'll learn how to do inventory and order stuff together. Because I don't have a clue."

"Maybe your father—"

"No. I promised them I would handle this. They've got their hands full with the restaurant. Besides, my mother…well, she's not really back to normal yet."

"I know she and Matt were close," Annie said. "I'm sure it'll take time for her to get over it." She stood. "I should go help Jessica get ready. Saturdays are busy."

Jordan nodded. "Brandon comes in at ten?"

"Yes. Staci works the afternoon."

"Okay."

Annie turned to go, but Jordan called her back.

"Annie?"

"Yes?"

"Thank you. I'd be lost if you weren't here."

Annie smiled. "I know." She paused before leaving. "And Jordan…we do have a dress code here. No slacks are allowed in the summer."

CHAPTER SIX

"What do you mean you don't have her number?"

Jessica shrugged. "I'm friends with her on Facebook though."

Jordan let out a heavy sigh. It was Thursday, and she hadn't heard from Annie all week. She had forgotten to get a phone number from her when they'd worked together on Sunday. But yesterday, Brandon had informed her that they were running low on several of the most popular T-shirts and their popcorn supply would not last through the weekend. And no, he didn't know where Matt got the popcorn from.

At first, she'd thought it was a terrible idea to have hot, buttery popcorn available where T-shirts were sold. But she was surprised at how careful most of the customers were, either wiping their fingers on the napkins provided or wiping their hands on their own clothes before picking up a T-shirt. And she had to admit, the smell of freshly popped corn was alluring. She'd found herself with a bag several times each day.

She went back into the office, trying to decide what to do. She'd been over Matt's books. It looked like there were only five vendors that he bought T-shirts from. She supposed she could call them up and find out which one produced the ones that Brandon said they were getting low on.

First things first. Popcorn. She went through the list of payables, one by one, finally seeing the one name that was not T-shirt or souvenir-related. Concession Stand Professionals. She clicked on it, surprised that Matt had taken the time to update the profile as thoroughly as he had. She followed the link to their website, putting in Matt's login and password. She was able to find his most recent order and simply clicked on that to reorder. Overnight shipping would get it to Rockport before the weekend.

"That was easy," she murmured. She hoped ordering the T-shirts would be as well.

Her cell phone chimed, and she glanced at it, feeling a surge of guilt as her mother's name popped up. She hadn't seen her parents all week.

"Hey, Mom," she answered. "It's nearly lunch. Aren't you busy?"

"Yes. But you haven't come by," her mother said in a slightly accusatory voice. "I wanted to check on you."

Jordan sighed. "I've been here until closing," she said. "Annie is out all this week, so I've been here all day, every day."

"I'm sorry you have to do that by yourself, Jordan. Matt... well, I guess that's why Matt slept there sometimes."

"I haven't resorted to that yet. I enjoy the quiet of the bay."

"Speaking of that, we can't wait to see what you've done at Pelican's Landing. Maria said you had some guys out there this week."

"Yes, trying to get the yard in shape," she said. She heard her father's voice in the background and smiled. "Sounds like you're in trouble."

"Yes. I'm getting behind on orders."

"Okay. Maybe Sunday evening you could come out," she suggested. "I could get some steaks. We'll grill out."

"That sounds good, honey. Let's plan on it."

Jordan twirled around in her chair, wishing there was a window in the office. Her office in Chicago was on the twenty-second floor. A large corner office with a great view. Unfortunately, she rarely took advantage of the view. She was surprised at how little she missed it, considering she spent far more hours there than at her condo, so much so that it was more of a home to her. She found she missed neither of them.

Her job was fast-paced and stressful. There was no downtime. She'd convinced herself she would be bored out of her mind here at Fat Larry's. That wasn't the case at all. She found she enjoyed the slower pace. She would give it a few weeks and learn the particulars of running the store. Then, if there were some changes she wanted to make, she'd pass it by her father. When she left at the end of summer, she wanted the store to be running on its own. That meant she'd have to hire a manager.

She thought it was a shame that Annie wouldn't be available for the job. She would be perfect. She already had the knowledge, she already knew the staff. She was older, she was mature. At least she'd be there full time during the summer. Maybe it would allow Jordan time to hire someone and let Annie train them. She wondered if there was anyone in Rockport who would fit the bill.

"Hey."

Jordan looked up, an involuntary smile lighting her face. "Hey. I was just thinking about you," she said as she took her reading glasses off and tossed them on the desk.

Annie walked into the office. "Good or bad?"

"Good. I miss you being here."

"Oh, yeah? You lost?"

Jordan laughed. "Well, I did manage to order some popcorn supplies on my own. Brandon said we were getting low."

"See? You don't need me."

"I do. We need T-shirts. How do we know which vendor supplies which ones?"

"Matt had a cheatsheet," Annie said.

"Not in that mass of papers I threw out, I hope?"

"I'm sure it was." Annie motioned for her to get up. "Lucky for you, I think he also kept a spreadsheet."

Jordan got out of the way and let Annie have the laptop. "What are you doing here? I thought I wouldn't see you until the weekend."

"My final was this morning. I had planned to stay at the library and study for the one tomorrow, but...well, I'm sick of studying," she said. "Here it is." She clicked on it, bringing up a rather crude spreadsheet. "Looks like it hasn't been updated since last summer, though."

She turned the laptop toward Jordan, and she picked up her glasses and slipped them on. There was a very short description of each T-shirt and the vendor who produced them. She frowned. "Does this mean anything to you?"

"Probably more than it means to you," Annie said.

"Great. Then I'll let Brandon tell you which ones we're low on and let you try to decipher Matt's description code." She paused. "That is, if you have time."

"I have time."

"Thanks. By the way, have you had lunch?"

"No. I came straight here from Corpus."

"Subway again? I can run out."

Annie nodded. "That would be good. Thank you." Annie reached for her purse, but Jordan stopped her.

"No. My treat. I'll be right back."

* * *

When Annie heard the outer door open, she assumed Jordan had returned with their lunch. Instead, she was shocked to see Derrick Dockery standing in the doorway, a solemn look on his face.

"I just heard," he said.

She raised her eyebrows.

"About Matt."

"Oh. Okay," she said.

"Why didn't you let me know? Me and Matt were friends," he said.

She recognized the tone of his voice and knew if she didn't stop things now they'd be headed for one of their classic arguments.

"First of all, it's no longer my responsibility to let you know these things. We've been divorced nearly four years. And secondly, you can't just show up here at my work," she said. "Especially back here in the office."

"Matt used to let me come back here."

"Matt is no longer here," she said.

He stared at her. "You've changed, Annie."

Good God. This again? "So you've been saying for the past ten years. What is it that you want?"

"I just got back on shore," he said. "I took a double shift. I thought maybe you and I could get together. Have dinner or something."

She shook her head, barely resisting rolling her eyes at him. "Are you in between dates again? What happened with that girl from Aransas Pass?"

"That didn't work out. She didn't like my shift work."

"Imagine that," she said dryly.

"So? Dinner?"

"No, Derrick. I'm not having dinner with you."

"Come on, Annie. One dinner."

There was movement behind him and Annie saw that Jordan had returned. She shook her head again. "No, Derrick."

He stepped closer and she noticed his dirty clothes. A flash from the past came back to her and she remembered how she'd used to make him strip off his clothes before coming in the house. The first few months of their marriage, it had become a game that turned into sex. Ten days apart, he would want to spend the first two back making love. She quickly learned not to be quite as strict with her laundry rules. Even then, a few months after their marriage, she had been searching for excuses not to have sex with him. God, why had it taken her nearly six years to divorce him?

"Are you afraid, Annie? Afraid that old attraction will still be there?"

At that, she laughed, unable to contain it. "I can assure you...no."

"I think you *are* afraid."

"Let's don't play this game, Derrick. I'm not going out with you. I'm sorry you're in between girlfriends right now, but I'm not your fallback." She looked past Derrick, seeing Jordan standing there, blatantly listening. "Now, my boss is here. You really need to go."

"Boss?" He spun around. "Who are you?"

Jordan stepped into the office, still holding the two sandwiches. "No, actually, the question is...who are *you* and why are you in my office?"

Annie was surprised that Derrick seemed to actually bristle at the question.

"I'm Derrick Dockery. Annie's husband."

"Oh, Derrick...*please*," Annie murmured.

"Annie's last name is Thomas, and I'm quite certain she told me she was not married."

Derrick gave a quick laugh. "Actually, I'm trying to win her back," he said.

Annie stood up. "Okay. Enough." She pointed to the door. "Out."

But Derrick's gaze was still focused on Jordan. "You look familiar."

"Jordan Sims. Matt's sister."

Derrick nodded. "Right. I remember you from high school."

"I'm sorry, but I don't remember you."

"Matt and I were friends. I was a year ahead of him in school. I used to see you out at the beach house sometimes," he continued.

Annie gave an apologetic look at Jordan before pushing by her and grabbing Derrick by the arm.

"Time to go," she said pointedly. "I have work to do."

He nodded. "Okay, well maybe some other time. I really want to get together."

She ushered him out into the store. "Goodbye, Derrick."

"What about over the weekend?"

"Really, Derrick…no."

She spun on her heels, leaving him standing there. He had some nerve, she'd give him that. Did he really think she'd have dinner with him? God, she hated when he wasn't dating anyone. For some reason, he thought he still had a claim to her.

Jordan was unwrapping her sandwich when she got back. Annie touched her shoulder as she passed by, resuming her seat behind the desk.

"I'm sorry," she said. "Derrick has no sense of proper divorce etiquette."

Jordan laughed. "So that's the ex, huh?"

"In all his glory, yes," she said as she unwrapped her own sandwich. "Thanks for this."

"Sure." Jordan took a bite from her sandwich, then stood, going out to the fridge. She returned with two water bottles. "I'm surprised he remembered me. I have absolutely no recollection of him."

"Derrick is forgettable that way," she said without thinking.

"So he's trying to win you back?"

"God, he's out of his mind," she said. "He got back on shore and only now found out about Matt's accident," she explained. "He's not dating anyone right now so he thinks I'm fair game."

Jordan stared at her for a moment. "I can't see you two together."

Annie nodded. "I know. I was young and stupid. And my mother loved Derrick. Still does. Derrick's parents and mine get together for dinner all the time." She took a bite of the sandwich, chewing quickly. "Considering how volatile the divorce was, it's very strange. I can picture the four of them plotting how to get me and Derrick back together."

"So your parents weren't in favor of the divorce?"

"No. Not at all. I had no support from them. In fact, at first, they refused to let me move back in with them, thinking I would stay with Derrick." She laughed. "Only the fear of the whole town knowing that I was living out at the Surf Court Motel changed their minds."

"Surf Court? Is that thing still standing?"

"No. It was condemned a few years ago. They tore it down. The city bought the lot and there's a park there now with a fishing pier."

Jordan nodded. "Quite a bit has changed around town."

"How long has it been since you've been back?"

"Six years."

"Wow."

"Yeah. Time kinda got away from me."

Annie nodded but didn't comment. She liked Jordan. Even though she didn't know much about her, Matt had mentioned her name frequently. She couldn't imagine being away for six years. Even though she had...well, *issues* with her own parents, she still wouldn't stay away.

Her gaze slid to the sofa and she looked away quickly. She wondered if she could talk Jordan into replacing the sofa. She couldn't look at it without remembering...*that night.*

"What?"

Annie looked up. "What?"

Jordan raised one eyebrow. "You looked at the sofa, you blushed, you frowned and then you looked away."

Annie felt her face turn red. "Are you always this observant?"

"Yes."

Annie gave her a fake smile, then took a large bite from her sandwich.

CHAPTER SEVEN

"Your mother says you've hired Annie Thomas as office manager."

Jordan handed her father a cold bottle of beer, then twisted the top on her own. Her mother was inside putting together a salad for their dinner.

"Yes. That's okay, isn't it?"

He nodded. "The store is yours to run," he said. "I don't have time for it."

Jordan pulled the string on the ceiling fan, then sat down beside her father. It had been a warm day, but the evening breeze had picked up and it was pleasant out on the deck. She loved it out here. She guessed that even during the brutal days of July and August, she'd prefer to have her meals outside.

She glanced over at her father. He rarely took the time to relax and was at the restaurant seven days a week. Over the years, he'd assembled a good staff and she wondered why he didn't slow down more. Maybe she got her work ethic from him. But he was relaxed now, she noted. His floral shorts were a bit gaudy and the Fat Larry T-shirt was snug against his ample stomach, but he had a peaceful look on his face.

"How's Mom been?" she asked.

He didn't pretend not to know what she meant. "She still cries at night," he said. "I know it takes time, but…I worry she won't get over this."

"And what about you?" she asked gently.

"What about me?"

"You've been so…so *strong* these past few weeks. You didn't hardly miss a day at the restaurant," she said.

"It's our livelihood. I can't just walk away because—"

"Because your son died?"

He looked at her sharply. "I have responsibilities, Jordan."

"At least Mom is letting her grief out. Have you even shed a tear?"

He stood up quickly, going to the railing. Was she out of line? Perhaps. But she'd not seen him shed a single tear, not even at the funeral. He was going on about his business as if Matt was coming back some day.

"My son died."

Jordan went to stand beside him. "Yes. Your son died. My brother died."

"I keep expecting him to barge into the kitchen at the restaurant and steal a fish fillet off a plate we're about to serve," he said with a shaky laugh. "Wearing one of those tie-dyed T-shirts he liked so." He turned to her. "Or him out there," he said, motioning to the bay. "Buzzing around on those Jet Skis while your mother and I entertained whatever gal he'd invited over for dinner."

"I'm so sorry, Dad."

He put his arm around her shoulder and pulled her closer. "Yeah. Me too. Life…well, you never know. We should all live as freely as Matt did. He liked to have fun. He didn't stress out about anything."

"No. No, he didn't."

Her father turned to her again. "It's not just your mom who cries at night."

She nodded, then leaned closer and kissed his cheek. "I'm sorry I haven't been around much, Dad."

"You're here now."

CHAPTER EIGHT

Annie barely made it to the toilet before she threw up. She held her stomach with both hands, waiting for the churning to pass.

"What the hell is wrong with me?"

It was the third day in a row where she'd been nauseous. Something she ate? But why was it only in the morning?

As she knelt beside the toilet, her eyes widened.

"Oh, dear God...*no*," she whispered. "Please no."

Before that thought could sink in, she vomited again. She wiped her mouth with the back of her hand, then rubbed her forehead. Okay, yes, she was late. Her period should have been last week. Maybe even the week before that, she thought. But the stress of Matt's death, the funeral, finals, starting a new job as office manager...all of that contributed to her being late. Surely.

"Oh, dear God," she murmured again.

She sat down, her back against the wall as she reached out to flush the toilet. "I can't be pregnant. I just can't be."

Can I?

She panicked. Should she call her mother? *God, no.* What about Suzanne? *Definitely no.*

She leaned her head against the wall. Should she call Jordan? She closed her eyes. *No.*

"Do the sensible thing, Annie. You pee on a stick and pray it's not positive."

She got up on shaky legs and stumbled back into her bedroom. Both of her parents were already at work, thankfully. And Jordan didn't expect her in until noon. She'd drive to Aransas Pass. No way could she buy a pregnancy test here in Rockport. Her mother would know about it before she even had a chance to pee on the damn thing.

* * *

Jordan glanced into the office, expecting to find Annie in there. It was after twelve and she was never late. She went to the fridge and took out the two sandwiches. As had been the norm for the last two weeks, on the days when Annie came in at noon, Jordan had Subway for their lunch.

Maybe it was because Annie was closer in age to her than anyone else, but she felt completely at ease around her. The others...not so much. Jessica was scared of her, she knew. And Staci, while friendly, never had much to say. Brandon was talkative and actually kind of playful, but still, he was all of twenty-three. The two new high school students they'd hired only worked weekends for now. They still had another week of school before they'd start coming in during the week.

She took the sandwiches into the office. The chair was pushed back so she knew Annie had been there. Today they were going to tackle the summer inventory. It should have been done a week ago.

She went back outside, frowning. Where the hell was Annie? She was about to go back into the office to wait for her when she heard a thud coming from the bathroom. She walked closer to the door, listening. Silence. She glanced down, seeing a light on inside. It had to be Annie. Well, she'd give her some privacy.

She turned to walk away. That was, until she heard another thud against the door. It sounded almost as if someone—Annie—was slowly banging their head against the door.

She raised her hand to knock, then paused. Then she knocked anyway.

"Annie? You okay?" She thought she heard crying and reached for the doorknob. It was locked. "Annie?"

She heard the lock turn and quickly opened the door. She was shocked to find Annie crying.

"What's wrong? Are you hurt?"

Annie met her eyes. "Oh, God...it's blue."

Jordan frowned. "Blue? What?"

Annie held up a plastic stick as tears streamed down her face. "It's...it's freaking blue."

Jordan didn't understand and took the stick from her. She looked at it, then back at Annie. "Pregnancy test?"

Annie nodded.

"And blue...is not good, I take it?"

Annie shook her head. "It's *so* not good. I'm pregnant." She met Jordan's gaze. "Jesus God, I'm *pregnant*," she sobbed.

Jordan didn't know what to do, so she opened her arms and Annie fell into them, sinking against her, her sobs coming harder now. Jordan folded her up, holding her tight.

"It'll be okay," she murmured.

"No. No, it won't," Annie mumbled against her chest. "It won't be okay."

CHAPTER NINE

Annie dreaded this conversation more than she'd dreaded anything else in her life. Even telling her parents she was going to divorce Derrick paled in comparison to this. At least it was only her mother. Her father wouldn't be home for at least another hour.

Her mother was in the kitchen starting dinner and Annie stood at the door, contemplating running back to her room and doing this another day. But another day wouldn't alleviate the stress that had settled upon her. As Jordan had said, just tell them and get it over with. It wasn't like she was a teenager, for God's sake.

"Mom?"

Her mother turned from the sink where she'd been washing the potatoes. "Annie, good. You can help me with dinner. The broccoli and cauliflower need to be washed," she said, pointing to the vegetables beside the sink. "I'll peel these."

Annie took a deep breath. "Actually, I need to talk to you," she said.

Her mother looked up. "Can you talk and wash at the same time? Your father will be home soon."

Annie swallowed, staring at the cauliflower. "I'm sure I could," she said. "But I don't really want to."

Her mother stopped in midstream, staring at her. "What is wrong with you?"

"Yeah…well…I'm kinda…kinda pregnant," she said, pulling her eyes away from her mother.

Silence greeted that statement for a good thirty seconds. Then her mother dropped the potato into the sink.

"You're…*what*?"

Annie looked up. "I'm pretty sure you heard me."

Her mother's hand flew to her chest. "*Pregnant*? Is it Derrick?"

"Derrick?" she asked, feeling her face scrunch into a frown. "God, no. Why would it be Derrick?"

"You're pregnant? And it's *not* Derrick?"

"Mom, no, it's not Derrick." She narrowed her eyes and she shook her head. "In case you've forgotten, we divorced about four years ago."

Her mother raised both hands into the air. "So…who's the father then, if not Derrick? I can't wait to hear *this*."

Annie clenched her jaw. "It doesn't really matter who the father is," she said. "I just thought you—"

"Of course it matters," her mother spat. "Or will you have an abortion?" Her mother nodded. "Yes. Yes, I think that's the best choice, Annie. An abortion. Don't you?"

Annie stared at her in disbelief. "Mom, for the last umpteen elections you've voted for candidates who were pro-life and against abortions. How can you possibly suggest that I have one?"

"It's different," she said. "This is different."

Annie shook her head. "Different? How?"

"Annie…you're living at home with your parents," she said. "You have no husband, you have no job. What are you going to do when you have this baby? Do you expect *me* to raise it?"

Annie squared her shoulders. "By no means," she said. "And I do have a job. And after my student teaching next spring, I'll have a job at the school."

"Do you really think they'll still hire you? An unwed mother? Is that a good example to set for these children?" Her mother grabbed her arms. "You're pregnant, Annie. Derrick is here. He's single. This is a perfect opportunity for you. Why don't you—"

Annie pulled away from her. "Mom, really, you've got to get over Derrick. I'm *not* going back to him."

"Then who? Who will you go to?" Her mother threw up her arms. "I can't *believe* this. You *do* know how this happens, don't you?"

"Are you trying to be funny?"

Her mother stared at her. "I wasn't even aware that you were dating anyone."

"I'm not."

"Then what?" But her mother shook her head. "No. I don't want to know." She touched her forehead and closed her eyes. "This is so depressing. And your father will have a coronary, I'm sure."

"I'm sure he won't," she said. She grabbed the bridge of her nose and squeezed. "I've got to…go by the store," she lied. "I'm sure we'll talk about this later."

"Well, I'm sure we will," her mother said. "You can't drop this bombshell and think it's over and done with. I mean, whatever in the world will the neighbors think? What about the people at church? How can I explain this?"

Annie sighed. "Tell them I'm a heathen," she said as she went back to her room.

Common sense told her to stay put. It would be dark in an hour. But the prospect of having dinner with her parents after her mother had filled her father in on…well, on her *condition*… wasn't appealing in the least. And her stomach warned her that she probably shouldn't eat anyway.

Her lone safe haven was Fat Larry's, but she knew the store would be closing soon. She could always drive out to the bay. Jordan wouldn't turn her away.

With that thought, she grabbed her keys and slammed her bedroom door. Her mother was again hovering over the sink, washing the broccoli and cauliflower that she had not.

"I'm heading out," she said.

"Dinner will be ready in—"

"Don't wait for me," Annie said quickly.

She realized how mad her mother was when she didn't protest that statement. She hurried to her car, wanting to get out of there before her father got home. She sped away, heading toward Fulton. She'd take the road along the bay, hoping to relax. She lowered all four windows in the car, breathing deeply of the salty air as it blew in. The road was busy and several cars were pulled off to the side, the occupants holding up binoculars as they scanned for birds in the waning twilight. As the road twisted around the bay, she turned, crossing over the highway and heading to the north to Copano Bay where Matt's beach house was. Well, Jordan's house now, she supposed.

She'd been out there only a couple of times. Matt had made it a point to have an office party each summer. They'd close early on a Sunday and he'd have them all out. The margarita machine was the hit of the party...that and the Jet Skis. And the buffet. Everything that his parents' restaurant served, he'd have for them. Fun times.

Yes, Matt had been fun. Was that why she'd slept with him? Because he was fun? No, of course not. She wasn't like that. She didn't sleep around. Which was really the problem, wasn't it? Couldn't she be like other women? Go out with a guy, sleep with him, have fun...no commitments. Like the guy she'd met in one of her classes...Jason. She'd gone out with him a few times, but when she'd made it clear that she wasn't interested in sex with him, he'd moved on to someone else.

He was cute. He simply didn't...didn't *stir* anything in her. She blew out her breath. It wasn't like Matt stirred anything either. But it had been a stormy April night and the prospect of going home to her parents was simply too disheartening at the time. She wanted to *do* something. She wanted to be a twenty-nine-year-old single woman. Not a twenty-nine-year-old divorced woman living at home with her parents.

"So let's have sex with Matt Sims," she murmured. And why the *hell* didn't she insist he use a condom?

Because getting pregnant never once entered her mind.

She turned onto Bayside, trying to remember which side street to take. When she saw Pelican Drive, she turned there. It was almost full dark now and her headlights splashed across the oak trees that lined the street on both sides. She saw the entrance to the driveway and smiled at the sign. *Pelican's Landing.* Fat Larry—well, a mini version of Fat Larry—was perched importantly on top of the marker.

She drove on, the winding lane ending at the carport. But it wasn't Jordan's rental car that was parked there. Instead, it was a newer model SUV. Maybe Jordan had company. She should have called first. She was about to do that when she saw Jordan step out on the porch and wave at her.

"I should have called," Annie apologized.

"No problem. Come on in," Jordan offered.

Annie pointed at the SUV. "Yours?"

"I'm leasing it," Jordan said. "A lot cheaper than the rental car."

Annie stood under the porch light and Jordan studied her. Annie finally nodded.

"Yes. I told my mother."

Jordan drew her inside and closed the door. "And? Was it as bad as you expected?"

"Yes. She hates me." She followed Jordan out to the deck where a bottle of wine and a lone wineglass sat on the table. There was no evidence of dinner.

"I'm sure she doesn't," Jordan said as she sat down. "I used to think my mother hated me too."

Annie frowned. "Why?"

Jordan shrugged. "Because I'm gay. I thought she would hate me for sure. I convinced myself that her tears were because she hated me."

Annie's mouth dropped open as she sank into a chair. "You're gay?"

"What? You didn't know?"

Annie shook her head. "No. Matt never said anything and… well, it never occurred to me, I guess." Annie leaned forward. "You don't…look gay."

Jordan laughed. "What does gay look like?"

"I don't know. Short hair, masculine, men's clothes."

Jordan laughed again. "That's a really old stereotype," she said. "Besides, my hair is fairly short."

"It's not short. It's the same length as mine."

Jordan's eyes widened in mock surprise. "Oh my God! Are you gay too?"

Annie laughed. "I wish. Then I wouldn't be pregnant. Of course, I know my mother would hate me for sure in that case."

Jordan poured wine into the glass, then looked at Annie. "I'd offer you some, but, pregnant and all."

Annie sighed. "I know."

"So what happened with your mother? She doesn't like the thought of being a grandmother?"

"Oh, she would love it. If only a husband came with it," she said. "And, you know, I'm still in college, I live with them, my sole source of income is Fat Larry." Annie met her eyes. "She wants me to have an abortion."

Jordan gasped. "No. You're not, are you?"

Annie shook her head. "No. I couldn't. But I'm going to have to find a place to live. Some cheap apartment or something. I can't go through this with her. Not for nine months. She'll drive me crazy. She's already suggested I get back with Derrick."

"Get back with him? Because you're pregnant?"

"I told you, she loves him."

"Maybe she should marry him."

Annie laughed. "Perhaps I'll suggest that to her the next time she brings it up."

Jordan leaned back in her chair, stretching her bare legs out and resting them on one of the empty chairs at the table. It was the most casual Annie had seen her. Even though she'd mostly stopped wearing business suits to the store, she'd yet to show up in shorts. Slacks and the occasional pair of jeans, but never shorts. Jordan had nice legs. She wondered why she kept them covered.

"What?"

Annie looked up. "What?"

"You were staring."

"Oh. I was looking at your legs." She then blushed as she realized how that sounded. "I mean—"

"Should I be worried?" Jordan teased.

"Why don't you wear shorts to the store?"

"Because these are the only pair I have. I packed in a hurry. I only brought a few suits with me and some dress clothes," she said. "I'd considered having some of my things shipped down here, but I think it would be as easy to buy new stuff. I don't exactly have beachwear in my closet."

"You always wear suits to work?"

"Yes. Always."

"I don't think I could stand that," she said.

Jordan shrugged. "I'm used to it now." She twirled the wine in her glass. "Have you had dinner?"

"No. My mother...well, I told her not to wait on me." She looked questioningly at Jordan. "Have you?"

"No. I don't really have anything here. I need to go shopping. Clothes and groceries," she said. "I can't keep eating at my parents' restaurant. I'll gain thirty pounds before the summer is over."

"We could order a pizza," Annie suggested. She wondered how that would set with her stomach. So far, her nausea only appeared in the mornings.

"Sounds good to me," Jordan said. "Any preference?"

"I like everything."

Jordan pulled out her phone. "Who delivers?"

"I'll call. There's a local place in Fulton that's pretty good," Annie said. "Unless you'd prefer one of the chains."

Jordan looked at her skeptically. "I'm from Chicago. It's sacrilege to get pizza from a chain."

Forty minutes later, the wine had been replaced with water bottles and they didn't bother with plates as they both ate directly from the box.

"This is really good," Jordan said. "Not classic deep dish, but good."

"Glad you like it," she said. Gino's was her very favorite place to eat so she was pleased that Jordan seemed to enjoy the pizza.

Their conversation drifted to less personal things besides her pregnancy and she enjoyed the stories Jordan told about spending lazy summer days out here at Pelican's Landing.

"How did it get its name?"

"My grandmother. My grandfather was obsessed with fishing. So before they even built the house, they built a pier out into the bay so he could fish. It was one of the first piers out here at that time. She said on any given day, there'd be twenty or thirty pelicans on it."

"Matt never mentioned them. Are they still alive?"

"No. He died suddenly, back when I was first starting college. And my grandmother died about six years ago."

"You said you'd been away six years," Annie reminded her. "Was that the last time you came?"

Jordan nodded. "Yeah. I came for her funeral."

Annie met her eyes. "And then you came back for Matt's."

"Yeah. Like I said, the years just kinda got away from me."

"Do you miss Chicago? The big city?"

"Not really. And since I haven't heard from my office, I guess they don't miss me."

The large pizza they'd ordered only had two remaining pieces left. Maybe it was simply the thought that she was pregnant but Annie had to talk herself out of reaching for one of them. She couldn't possibly still be hungry.

"Why don't you take this with you?" Jordan offered. "Lunch tomorrow."

"You don't mind?"

"No. You'll be on your own anyway."

"Where will you be?"

"I think I'm going to Corpus. Need to do some clothes shopping."

"And the grocery store," Annie added as a reminder. "The house seems really different. What have you done?"

"You mean besides clean it?"

Annie laughed. "Yeah, Matt was a bit of a slob, wasn't he?"

Jordan nodded. "His things, well, I took them to my parents' house. Mom's not ready to part with them yet. His clothes have all gone to Goodwill. And I rearranged the living room to open up the view a bit more."

"I've only been here a couple of times. It looks nice."

"Oh, yeah? Were you one of the girls my parents had to entertain while Matt played on the water?"

"No. Matt had a party out here the last two summers. We'd close the store early on a Sunday and he'd bring in food from the restaurant. And a margarita machine," she added with a smile.

"Most of them aren't even old enough to drink."

"Yeah. Matt didn't really care."

"So are you saying I need to do the same thing?"

"If you want them to like you, you should."

Jordan laughed. "That's all it'll take? A margarita machine?"

"Well, they're still not over the whole punch-clock thing. It might take more than that," she teased.

Jordan wrapped up the pizza for her while Annie leaned against the counter, watching her. The kitchen was neat and tidy…spotless, actually. She'd learned in the last month that Jordan was a neat freak. Apparently, that didn't only pertain to the office.

"Here you go," Jordan said.

Annie took the pizza. "Thanks. I hope I make it home with them." She laughed. "Maybe it's only my imagination, but I've been ravenous lately."

Jordan's eyes swept over her body, and Annie felt an odd flutter in her stomach as Jordan's gaze settled on her face again.

"You're thin, small frame. You probably won't gain much weight," Jordan said.

"You think not? I hope you're right. I hope I take after my mother in that regard. She stayed thin during her pregnancy too." Annie laughed. "I've already had visions of my toes swelling up like Vienna sausages."

Jordan laughed too. "Do you have sisters to compare it to?"

Annie shook her head. "No. There's only me. Not for lack of trying, my dad likes to say."

"Well, if you're their only child, they won't turn their backs on you."

"Oh, I know. But do I want to put up with *hell* for nine months?" she said with a laugh. "Thank you, Jordan. For letting me come out here uninvited. It's been stress-free and I feel so much better."

"You're welcome." Jordan led her to the door, then paused before opening it. "You know, I've got room here."

"Room?"

"If you want to stay here," Jordan clarified. "Instead of the Surf Court Motel."

Annie laughed at her reference to the old condemned motel. "I appreciate the offer, but I couldn't possibly impose on you like that."

Jordan's expression turned serious. "I wouldn't have offered if it was going to be an imposition," she said. "There's an extra bedroom and bath that I'm not using. Besides, when I head back to Chicago, maybe you could rent the place from my parents or something."

Annie was stunned by her offer. "Are you sure?"

Jordan nodded. "We get along fine. I like you. It would be nice to have someone to share dinner with."

"We also work together," Annie said. "Is that too much?"

"Well, since you're the office manager and things are running smoothly, I'm only going to pop in from time to time. And when you start back to college, we'll have to hire someone else anyway."

"You're really going to stay through summer?"

"I took a leave of absence. I think my job is safe if I head back by September. When do classes start for you?"

"Last week in August."

"Perfect. We'll hire someone the first of August and you can train them," Jordan said. "Provided my father will go for that."

"What do you mean?"

"Family business. He's not big on outsiders running things. That's why he's at the restaurant as much as he is."

They stepped out onto the porch and Jordan turned the light off as moths were buzzing around their heads.

"Smells like rain," Annie noted. "I love spring storms."

"First week in June…can we still say spring?"

"Yes. We don't want to rush summer." Annie turned to her. "I can't believe it's been six weeks since Matt's been gone. Six weeks tomorrow."

"I know. And the world just keeps on turning, doesn't it?" Jordan shoved her hands into the pockets of her shorts. "My offer is genuine, Annie. You're welcome to stay here."

Annie tried to catch her eyes in the shadows but couldn't. She was surprised at how easy it was to answer her.

"I accept."

CHAPTER TEN

Jordan nodded at a couple of waitresses as she slipped back into the kitchen. It was barely five and the dinner rush had not yet started. Still, her father was busy with his fish and her mother was tapping on the computer that held the online orders.

"Hey, Mom," she said as she leaned against the counter.

Her mother stared at her. "What happened to you?"

Jordan raised her eyebrows questioningly.

Her mother swept her hand toward her. "Did you rob a clothing store?"

Jordan laughed. "It probably would have been less stressful than my shopping trip to the mall." She absolutely hated shopping. It was one reason all her business suits were practically the same. All she did was mix and match and change blouses. Most of her clothes she ordered without stepping foot inside a store.

"You knew you would be staying here this summer. You should have brought more clothes."

"Yes, well, I don't have a lot of clothes that would be appropriate for Rockport," she said. "Annie told me I was way

overdressed for Fat Larry's." Of course, she knew she was.
Rockport was summertime casual, for residents and tourists
alike. She, however, had dressed as if she was heading up to her
high-rise office in Chicago, ready to do battle for multimillion-
dollar accounts.

"Well, you look nice," her mother said. "Did you come for
dinner?"

"I thought we could visit before the rush," she said. "Do you
have time?"

"Yes. Grab us some tea. I'll have Brenda take over the
orders."

Jordan had just sat down with their drinks when someone
brought over a basket of freshly baked onion and garlic biscuits.
They were still glistening with melted butter and she reached
for one.

"Thanks," she said before taking a bite. "God, that's sinful."

"Aren't they?"

"You want one?" she asked her mother.

"No. You know I don't eat anything from here."

"I know. And after all these years, Dad still has an appetite
for fish. If I had to cook it every single day, I'd never touch it."

Her mother took a sip from her tea. "Are things okay at the
store?"

"Yes. Fine." Jordan licked her fingers, then wiped them on a
napkin. "The hardest part is getting a handle on the inventory
and making sure orders are placed. I'm sure Matt had a system,
but I can't seem to find it."

Her mother smiled at the mention of Matt's name and
Jordan wondered if her mother was getting past her constant
grieving. Normally, a mention of his name brought a shadow of
sadness to her face, not a smile.

"Your father used to say the same thing," she said. "I think
that's one reason he was so pleased you were willing to take
over. He didn't have a clue as to what Matt's system was."

"Annie's been a big help," Jordan said. "She would make a
good permanent manager. But since she's about through with
college, I guess she's pretty much set on teaching."

"Matt always spoke highly of her. I'm glad she's helping you out."

Jordan nodded. "Speaking of that, I wanted to return the favor," she said. "So I offered for her to move in at Pelican's Landing."

Her mother's eyes widened. "Move in? Why?"

"She lives at home with her parents."

"And?"

"Well, and she's kinda pregnant and it's not sitting too well with her mother. So…"

Her mother leaned closer. "How is someone *kinda* pregnant?"

Jordan shrugged. "Annie uses that word. I guess it's become habit. Anyway, I wanted to let you know that I offered her a place to stay. That's okay, isn't it?"

Her mother wiped a droplet of water from her glass. "Of course, Jordan. Treat the house like it's your own. But she's okay with…well, with everything?"

"What do you mean?"

"I mean, does she know you're…gay?" she asked, the last word barely more than a whisper.

Jordan smiled. "Yeah, she knows. It's not contagious. I think she'll be safe."

Her mother blushed. "That's not what I meant and you know it. But I know Clara. She's not going to—"

"Who's Clara?"

"Annie's mother."

"Annie's twenty-nine years old, Mom. I don't think she has to get her mother's approval."

"I know. I just don't want to get into the middle of a family tiff."

"That's none of our business," she said quickly. "Annie told me she was going to have to find a place to live so I offered the spare bedroom. It's no big deal. I just wanted to let you know."

Actually, it was a big deal. She'd surprised herself with the offer. She'd always lived alone. She was used to her own routine, used to her own company…used to being alone. But, hell, she liked Annie. They got along well and she thought of Annie as more of a friend than an employee.

"What will happen when you leave?"

Jordan shrugged. "Maybe she can rent it from you."

Her mother sighed. "I don't know, Jordan. I doubt your father will want someone living there who is not family. You know how he is."

"I know. But he's going to have the same problem with Fat Larry's. He's going to have to trust someone who isn't family. I can stay through August, then I'll have to head back. They won't hold my job forever."

"I thought you took a leave of absence."

"I did. But it's not indefinite, Mom."

Truth was, her being away from her job was giving an opening to Antonio, her assistant. He was ambitious and had made no effort to hide the fact that he wanted to move up in the company. What better way to prove himself? She was gone and he had yet to even call her. She'd voiced her concern to Peter, but he had assured her that her job was safe. Antonio was good, she'd give him that. But his personality was a bit abrasive, a point that wasn't lost on Peter.

"Well, we trust you, Jordan. Whatever you think is best, we'll go along with it."

"Thank you." Jordan reached for another biscuit. "How well do you know Annie?"

"Just from the store, really. Even though she and Matt were in the same grade, I don't recall her hanging out with him and his friends. Do you?"

Jordan shook her head. "No. But then I was older."

They were silent for a moment, then her mother reached out her hand and captured Jordan's. "Have I told you lately how glad I am that you're here?"

Jordan smiled. "I'm glad I'm here too." Then her smile faded. "I'm sorry that I wasn't around much before. I got used to…staying away, I guess."

Her mother nodded. "Yes, you did. And I'm sorry for my part in that."

Jordan squeezed her hand. "We can't get those years back, Mom, but maybe going forward, I can spend more time here."

"We'd like that." Her mother released her hand. "Now, I better get back to work before your father comes looking for me." She paused. "Are you staying for dinner?"

"I was. But after two of these, I better skip fried food. I need to go to the grocery store anyway. I'll pick something up."

Her mother leaned down and kissed her cheek. "I love you, Jordan. I don't say it nearly enough."

Jordan felt her eyes dampen with tears. "I love you too."

CHAPTER ELEVEN

Annie threw up her hands in frustration. "What do you want me to do? You're embarrassed to have me living here, yet you don't want me to move out."

"Not move in with a complete stranger," her mother said loudly.

"Jordan is not a stranger," Annie said as she piled more clothes into her bag.

"She's a stranger to me."

"Lucky for you, you're not the one moving in with her," Annie shot back. They'd been arguing over this for the past two days.

"I just don't understand you. Getting pregnant in the first place," her mother said with a shake of her head. "That's just—"

Annie held up her hand, stopping her mother. "Please. We've been over this. I know you're disappointed in me. *I'm* disappointed in me too," she said. "But continuing to hash it over will not change anything. So for both of our sanities, I think it's best that I don't live here." She squared her shoulders, weary of this conversation. "Jordan was kind enough to offer me a place to live. She's not going to charge me rent. I'll help with the groceries, that's it. So you don't need to worry about me."

"Of course I'll worry about you. I don't know this woman, but I know *of* her," she said.

"What's that supposed to mean?"

"You have no business living with her. That's what that means."

Annie laughed, finally realizing what her mother was trying to say. "You mean because she's a lesbian?"

"So the rumors are true then?"

"Yes."

"Then why would you live with her?"

Annie paused. "I like her. She's nice. We get along great." She shrugged. "And like I said, she's not charging me rent."

"Maybe because she expects you to pay in other ways," her mother said quietly.

Annie stared at her. "Seriously? *That's* what you're worried about?"

"You don't know her. She might—"

"Mom, you know her parents. You knew Matt. They're good people. Jordan is too. Now quit being ridiculous about it."

"I think we should at least meet her first."

Annie laughed and shook her head. "Why would I subject Jordan to that?" She went to her mother and took both of her hands in her own. "Mom, I'm twenty-nine years old. I can handle this. And while I appreciate all you and Dad have done for me, it's time I moved out. Getting pregnant was not something I ever expected. But it's my problem, not yours."

"Annie, we'd never—"

"I know you wouldn't. But it's time. I need to do this, Mom. I need some semblance of independence. I'm working full time this summer. I'll be able to save a lot of money so that I can afford something on my own next year."

"So you and…your baby will live in a cheap apartment or something? Is that what you're striving for? You haven't even told us who the father is. Have you told him? Is he not going to help with this?" Her mother stared at her. "Do you even *know* who the father is?"

Annie looked away. "Of course I know who the father is."

"And?"

"And what? I'm handling it, Mom," she said, refusing to fight with her anymore. "Now, let me finish."

Her mother turned and walked away without another word, and Annie let out a sigh. Was she making a mistake by leaving the security of her parents' house? Even though her mother obviously wasn't happy with the situation, she would never kick her out. Would it be better to stay here until she had the baby?

She shook her head. She couldn't take another eight months of this. She knew her mother too well. Snide remarks would slip out, whether consciously or not. And then there would be the constant mention of Derrick and getting back with him. That in itself was enough to convince her to leave.

She paused, rubbing her hand across her belly. She didn't really feel any different. Well, other than being sick nearly every morning. But shouldn't she *feel* different? She wondered how soon it would be before she started showing. She hadn't told Suzanne yet. Because once she told Suzanne, Derrick would find out. Actually, she was surprised Derrick didn't already know. Unless her mother was simply too embarrassed by her pregnancy to tell Derrick's mother.

She stared up at the ceiling, then closed her eyes. What was she going to do? Eventually, she'd have to tell *someone* who the father was. Should she tell Jordan? Matt's parents? Would they even believe her?

She wiped impatiently at a tear that had fallen. Now was no time to start feeling sorry for herself. She had too much to do. Once she got settled in at Pelican's Landing, the first thing she had to do was find a doctor. Even though she'd gone through pregnancies with Macy and Suzanne, she knew very little about it. That was about to change.

CHAPTER TWELVE

"So she'd heard rumors, huh?" Jordan flipped the chicken over and turned the gas grill down.

"Yes. And when I told her you weren't charging me rent, she said that was because you expected me to pay in *other* ways."

Jordan laughed. "Well, sure. I expect you to cook."

Annie pointed at the grill. "You seem to be doing a good job," she said.

"I'm afraid this is it," she said. "I've done steaks, pork chops, chicken and even portabella mushrooms and squash. Other than that, I'm afraid anything else would have to come out of a box or a can." She smiled. "Well, I can do baked potatoes."

"Yes. I saw them in the oven," Annie said.

She added more wine to her glass, then looked at Annie apologetically as she watched. "Sorry. Would you rather I didn't drink wine?"

Annie shook her head. "I don't mind. Besides, I'm the one who's pregnant, not you."

"Yeah. Thank God." Annie had a thoughtful expression on her face, and Jordan arched an eyebrow questioningly.

Annie tilted her head. "When did you know you were gay?"

Jordan wasn't surprised by the question. She was curious though as to why Annie was asking it.

As if reading her mind, Annie added, "Because you don't have a gay vibe."

Jordan laughed. "And you know these vibes how?"

Annie smiled. "I watch *Ellen.*"

"Ah. Of course. Well, maybe it's because you've seen me in nothing but business suits and dress clothes," she said. "Maybe now that I've got a wardrobe full of shorts and jeans, I'll butch out a little bit for you."

Annie reached for her water bottle. "So? When did you know?"

Jordan shrugged. "Subconsciously, I guess I always knew. In reality, it was my junior year in high school. There was a sleepover, a slumber party type thing. After the first football game of the year, Friday night, we all went out for pizza. There were six of us. Then we went over to Beth's house for the weekend. They had a pool and it was still warm. We played games, gossiped, made a mess of her mother's kitchen at breakfast. And at night, we lit candles and laid in a circle, playing a vague game of Truth or Dare."

"Someone asked you?"

"No. Nothing like that. But I was next to Sherry. Sherry Bozart. And I looked into her eyes and felt something that I'd never felt before."

Annie leaned closer. "Sherry Bozart? The name doesn't ring a bell. Who did she marry?"

"No clue," she said. "But after that night, things started to make sense to me. It all came crashing down and I panicked."

"You didn't tell anyone?"

"Not a soul. And speaking of *Ellen*, it was the same year she came out on her show and everybody was talking about it. I was terrified I would say the wrong thing and my friends would find out."

"Did you date guys?"

"Sure. Had a boyfriend at the time. Like I said, it all made sense to me then. I broke up with him the next weekend."

"Were you sleeping together?"

Jordan laughed. "No. Doing everything *but* that." She gave an exaggerated shudder. "Gross."

Annie laughed too, but to Jordan's relief didn't ask any other questions. Jordan, however, had one for her.

"Are you ever going to tell me who the father is?"

Annie met her gaze. "I suppose I'm going to have to someday, yes."

"It isn't Derrick, is it?"

"God, no." Annie looked startled that she would even suggest that. "I didn't want to have sex with him when we were married. Why would I sleep with him now?"

Of course, that statement brought all sorts of questions to mind, but Annie pointed at the grill and Jordan turned, seeing smoke seeping out.

"I suppose it's time to rescue those," she said as she got up.

"I'll get the potatoes," Annie offered. "Or did you want to eat inside?"

"I prefer out here, if it's okay with you."

"Fine with me."

Conversation over dinner drifted to less personal things, and they ended the evening with a quick walk down to the pier.

"I've got to do something with this," Jordan said. "A lot of boards need to be replaced."

"Have you walked to the end?"

"Yes and it's a miracle it didn't collapse on me," she said. "I want to take the Jet Skis out for a spin too. My father said that Matt had them serviced in March so they should be good to go." She glanced at Annie. "Do you ride?"

Annie shook her head. "The only time I've been on one was at Matt's party last year. Brandon took me out and proceeded to dump me in the water after one spin. He was quite proud of himself."

"I'll take you out if you want," she said. "It's been years since I've been on one. I'm sure my speed will be more grandmother than teenager."

"Thanks. That would be fun."

CHAPTER THIRTEEN

Annie looked up from the computer when she heard someone clear her throat. She was shocked to see Suzanne staring at her. She'd been avoiding her for the last two weeks. She plastered a smile on her face now.

"Hey, stranger," she said.

"What? You start working full time and you don't have time for me anymore?"

"I'm sorry," she said. "I've had a lot going on."

"Well, how about I steal you away for lunch? Britney is with her grandmother today so I'm free."

Annie wasn't sure if she was prepared to face Suzanne yet, but she could think of no excuse to decline the offer.

"Sounds good," she said. "Give me a couple of minutes. I was about to place an order."

"Okay. I'll go rummage through your new T-shirts. Come find me."

Annie nodded and glanced at the screen, trying to remember what she was about to add to the order. Oh, yeah…flip-flops. Jordan's idea.

"Hey, you."

She smiled as Jordan sauntered into the office. She looked so much different now than when she'd first come to the store. The dress pants and business suits were replaced with shorts and Fat Larry T-shirts. She hadn't yet taken to wearing flip-flops, but the water sandals fit in quite nicely.

"Hey. You're early. Good."

"Good?"

"Suzanne is here. Wants to go to lunch," she said.

"Oh." Jordan raised her eyebrows. "You going to tell her?"

Annie took a deep breath. "I suppose." She finished the order and closed the laptop. "And don't forget, I have my first doctor's appointment tomorrow."

Jordan nodded. "You sure you don't want me to go with you?"

"Don't you think one of us should be here at the store? Besides, it's in Corpus."

"What about your mother?"

Annie shook her head. "She's still kinda not speaking to me."

"Well, she'll come around. Give her time."

"I know." Annie stood and walked around the desk, pausing to wrap her fingers around Jordan's arm and squeeze it lightly. "Thank you. See you later."

"Have fun."

Annie met her gaze and smiled. "If only."

She found Suzanne where she said she'd be and like most customers, Suzanne simply tossed the T-shirt she'd been looking at back on top of the others. Annie had to resist the urge to fold it up neatly again.

"Where to?"

"Mexican food," Suzanne said. "Let's go across the street to Pepe's."

Pepe's was crowded, as usual, but they were able to snag a table for two on the side patio. They had a view of the marina, but the June day was warm. Annie adjusted the colorful umbrella to shade them.

"So how's the new boss?" Suzanne asked as she added salt to the basket of warm chips that were placed between them.

"Jordan? She's great. Completely different personality than Matt, that's for sure."

Suzanne broke a chip in half before dunking it into the salsa. "How so?"

"Oh, she's more serious, more mature. Organized. Neat. Matt just did things on a whim. She doesn't have his playfulness, though. At least, not that she's shown."

"So you've been busy? I tried calling a couple of times."

"I know. I'm sorry I didn't call you back." Annie bit her lip, hesitating. "I kinda…well, I have some news."

"Oh, yeah?"

"Yeah. First of all, I moved out from my parents' house last week."

"You're kidding?"

"No. And I…I moved in with Jordan. To Matt's old place on the bay."

Suzanne's eyes widened slightly. "Why?"

"Well, my mother…she didn't take the news about me being pregnant very well."

Suzanne spit out the water she'd just taken a sip of. "*What? Pregnant?*"

Annie nodded. "It appears that way, yes."

Suzanne's hand touched her chest and for a few seconds she appeared speechless. Then she leaned closer, her voice a whisper. "Who's the father?"

"Matt."

"Oh, my God," she nearly shrieked. "You have *got* to be kidding me."

"I wish I was." She reached across the table and squeezed Suzanne's hand. "I haven't told anyone yet. About Matt, I mean. I know I have to, but the time hasn't been right."

"You haven't told his sister?"

"No. I don't want to just blurt it out."

Suzanne shook her head several times. "You realize Derrick is going to flip out, don't you? I mean…*flip out.*"

"I know. And when he finds out it was Matt, he's going to be doubly pissed. They were friends. He'll look at it as betrayal, even though we've been divorced four years." She pointed her finger at Suzanne. "And that's why I'm threatening you within an inch of your life," she said. "Because if you tell Derrick, I will *hunt* you down."

"I won't be the one to tell Derrick. I don't need that drama," Suzanne said with a wave of her hand.

"Promise?"

"Of course. But I am…well, I'm simply blown away." A smile lit her face. "I can't believe you're pregnant. This is so exciting!"

"Exciting? No, it's not. I'm not sure I really believe it." She pushed the chips aside. "I'm not through with college yet. I'm basically homeless. The father is…is deceased. My mother is not speaking to me. My father told me he was disappointed in me. So, no, it's not exciting in the least."

Suzanne waved her protest away. "Your mother is only worried about what the people at her church are going to say. Maybe now she'll quit badgering you to go to church with her."

Annie smiled. "I guess that's one way to look at it."

"So who's your doctor? This is going to be so much fun. I can't wait."

Annie should have known Suzanne would be happy for her. When they'd first gotten married and both Macy and Suzanne were pregnant, they had practically begged Annie to do the same. She'd told them she wasn't ready and they'd eventually let it drop. Truth was, she wasn't ready now either. She tried to let Suzanne's enthusiasm wash over her and it did.

A little.

"So what are you going to eat? Want to share nachos or something?"

"Are you kidding? I've been starving lately. I want, like, enchiladas or something. Beans, rice, the works."

"Don't go overboard," Suzanne warned. "That weight will just creep up on you."

"I don't care," she said. And at that moment, while perusing the enchilada platters on the menu, her potential weight gain was the least of her worries.

After their orders were taken and Suzanne's salsa bowl was refilled, she scooted her chair closer to Annie.

"So do you have a plan?"

Annie frowned. "A plan?"

"You know, after the baby is born. School, work. A place to live."

"Are you trying to depress me?" she asked.

"No, of course not. I'm just wondering what you're going to do."

"Well, I'm going to finish college, do my student teaching next spring, then start full time the next fall. That's still the plan. As far as where I'm going to live, I'll cross that bridge when I come to it."

Suzanne broke another chip in half before dipping it in the salsa. "Look, don't take this the wrong way," she said, "but have you considered Derrick?"

"Oh, God, not you too?"

"I'm just saying, he's still crazy about you. He would—"

"Suzanne, there's a reason we divorced, you know." She took a sip of water, staring at Suzanne. "Are you happy being married, Suzanne?"

Suzanne appeared startled by the question. "Why would you think I'm not happy?"

Annie shrugged. "I'm just…I'm wondering why you're happy and I never was. I mean, I don't know what went wrong with Derrick." She shook her head. "Well, I do know. I shouldn't have ever married him in the first place. I just…I got carried away with it all, I think."

"With what?"

"With all of us," she said. "He and Aaron and Chuck. You, me and Macy. Everything just piled on top of each other. They were best friends, we were best friends. His parents and my parents were friends. I got caught up in it all and I couldn't get out." She took another drink of her water, wondering where she was going with this. These thoughts were private, thoughts she'd not shared with anyone before. "I think I knew before we even got married that it wasn't the real thing for me, yet I went through with it," she admitted. "And after six months, I was certain that it wasn't for me. But no matter how unhappy I was, I pretended that I wasn't. Because I was caught up in the whole group thing. And I put up with it for six years. Six *years*."

"Oh, Annie. I could tell you weren't happy. I thought maybe if you had a kid—"

"Now that was the smartest thing I did...*not* getting pregnant. I'd still be married to him then, I'm sure. And I'd be miserable."

"So were you ever in love with him?"

"In love?" Annie shook her head. "No. No, I don't think so. Not that deep, crazy kind of love. He was just the guy I dated all through high school, the guy everyone assumed I would marry. Before I could even contemplate what was happening, I was standing in front of the preacher saying 'I do,' and then it was too late." She sighed. "I guess I'm telling you all of this so you won't have this hope that Derrick and I will get back together. Because it's not going to happen. Ever."

Suzanne nodded. "Okay. I won't bring it up again. I'm sorry. I thought it might be an option."

"It's not."

CHAPTER FOURTEEN

Jordan waited until Brandon had finished with his customer, then waved him back. The smile that was almost always on his face faltered a bit.

"You wanted to see me, boss?"

Jordan led him into the office. She had stopped asking him to call her "Jordan" instead of "boss." It had made no difference. He still called her "boss." She assumed it was because of her dress—the business suits. She'd hoped that once she started dressing like them, in shorts, that he would loosen up, but no.

She motioned to the visitor's chair. "Sit down," she said.

"Am I in trouble? Did I do something wrong?"

She stared at him. "I don't know. Did you?"

The color left his face. "I don't think so," he said.

She smiled, trying to get him to relax. "Then why do you look guilty?"

"Because this is like being called back to the principal's office. You *never* ask any of us to come back here."

She leaned her elbows on the desk. "Why are you here?"

He frowned. "What?"

"Here. At Fat Larry's. Annie tells me you have your degree."

"Yes."

"So?"

He shrugged. "I've worked here since high school," he said.

"Right. And now you have your degree. In fact, you got it in December."

"You don't like me working here?" he asked hesitantly.

"I love you working here. You're a natural with the customers. You're friendly. And you flirt just enough with the ladies but don't ever cross the line. At least, not that I've seen."

He actually blushed, and it made him look even more handsome, she noted.

"I guess I don't understand your line of questioning," he said.

"What are your goals, Brandon?"

He nodded. "Oh, I see. Is this like a…'where do you see yourself in five years?' kind of a thing?"

"Exactly."

He smiled and brushed his blond hair off his tanned face. "I'm just…you know, hanging out. Enjoying myself. I'm into sailboarding," he said. "So working here, the hours are flexible, I can still hit the water whenever I want."

"You have your degree. You work part-time. Your goal is… sailboarding?"

"Look, money is not that big a deal," he said. "I have a roommate. My Jeep is paid for." He glanced over his shoulder as if making sure they were still alone. "I have money," he said quietly. "My uncle…well, he paid for my college. Paid for my Jeep. He and my father were the only children and he never married. And I don't have any siblings." He paused. "He's kinda rich."

"And he gives you money?"

"Yeah. I'm on his payroll."

"Unbelievable," she murmured.

"Yeah. It's sweet."

"So if you've got it so sweet, why do you work here?"

"I love it here. Like I said, it's flexible. And I've got to do something productive with my life. I can't sailboard all day long." He paused. "Besides, I started working here in high school. This is like home to me."

She leaned back in her chair. "So if I offered you more money, that's not really an incentive to you, seeing as you've got another job that you don't actually have to work at."

"I'm always open for more money," he said with a smile. "What do you have in mind?"

She wondered if this was a good idea, but hell, she liked the guy. And she thought she could trust him. So, she gave voice to what she'd been contemplating for the last couple of weeks.

"Right now, Annie and I take turns closing the store. And I understand that before, Matt would always close."

"Yes. And?"

"And I want to train you to close. If it works out, I'll give you a raise." She shrugged. "I was going to offer you more hours too, but that might cut into your sailboarding," she said with a smile.

"Like close on my own?"

"Yes. Like be in charge of clearing out the cash register, reconciling the receipts, that sort of thing. Obviously, locking up and setting the alarm when you leave."

"Cool."

"Cool? You interested?"

"Sure. And I could take a few more hours too, boss."

"Great. We'll start training today."

CHAPTER FIFTEEN

Annie walked into the house, her hands loaded with three grocery bags, but Jordan was nowhere to be seen.

"Jordan? You around?" she called.

She put the perishables in the fridge, then peeked out onto the deck. It too was empty. She heard a splash in the water and looked past the railing of the deck, down to the pier. Jordan was out in the water. She took the stairs on the side of the deck, heading toward the bay. She stopped abruptly when she saw Jordan.

She was up to her waist in the water, wearing a bikini top, and it was the first time Annie had seen her this exposed. She looked stunning. Annie found herself staring. She shook it off, finally settling on her face. It was then she noticed the change.

"Oh, my God! You got a haircut," she exclaimed.

Jordan looked up and smiled before running a wet hand through her now shorter hair. "Yeah. Thought I'd butch out a little for you," she teased.

"It looks great," Annie said.

Jordan came out of the water, and Annie's gaze dropped to her waist, where she expected to see a bikini bottom to accompany the top. She was somewhat disappointed that wasn't the case. She blinked that thought away as water droplets ran down Jordan's flat stomach and onto the water shorts she had on.

"So what are you doing?" she asked.

"Seeing how bad the pier really is," Jordan said. "I thought maybe a few boards here and there could be replaced, but I think we'll have to redo the whole thing. Some of the pylons are rotted."

"Can you get to the Jet Skis?" she asked hopefully, remembering Jordan's offer of a ride.

"Yeah. I can walk in the bay if I have to. Maybe we'll take them out on Sunday."

Annie looked at her questioningly. "You going to close the store early?"

"No."

Annie frowned. "Wait a minute." She glanced at her watch. "What are you doing home anyway? Who's at the store?"

Jordan smiled. "I'm trusting Brandon to close."

"By himself? You only trained him yesterday," she reminded her.

"Yeah." Jordan shrugged. "He did fine. And it's not that hard. I told him if he doesn't screw anything up today, I'll up his hourly wage," Jordan said. "So, how was the doctor's visit?"

Annie sighed. "I've been poked and prodded, peed in a cup, gave blood and answered more questionnaires than I can possibly remember. But I like her, I guess. She's young."

"Good. How often do you have to see her?"

"Every four weeks for now," she said. "The next appointment won't be nearly this long, they tell me."

Jordan eyed her. "So? Are you excited yet?"

Annie smiled. "Excited? A little. Scared? A lot." She held up her hand. "Let's save baby talk for later. I thought I'd cook dinner," she said, remembering the reason she'd been looking for Jordan in the first place.

"Oh, yeah? Well, that was one of your alternate payment methods, wasn't it?" Jordan teased.

"Yes. My mother will be happy to hear that," she said with a quick smile. "I picked up some pork chops. I know how you like to grill."

Jordan walked beside her up the deck and playfully bumped her shoulder. "So *you* were going to cook, huh?"

"I'm making a very secret recipe. It involves potatoes and cheese and sour cream and it's way too fattening, but I'm having a craving. So yes, I'm cooking that. You are doing the chops. Deal?"

"I accept. Let me grab a shower first."

Annie nodded, her gaze following Jordan until she rounded the corner and went into her bedroom.

"What in the world is *wrong* with you?" she murmured to herself with a shake of her head. Her doctor did warn her of hormonal changes. She made no mention that she might suddenly start ogling her female boss's body.

* * *

Jordan got out of the shower and toweled her wet hair. She glanced in the mirror as she ran her hand through the shorter strands. The cut was a spur-of-the-moment decision, and she still couldn't quite believe she'd done it. One minute, she's standing outside the liquor store with her two bags of wine and the next, she's seated in a chair at Quick Clips asking for a "summer cut."

To be sure, it wasn't drastically short, just different. She'd always been a bit conservative in her dress, her appearance— nothing to call attention to herself. She wore the barest amount of makeup, minimal jewelry, gray or black business suits. Conservative.

Now here she was, wearing shorts and T-shirts to work, no makeup, no jewelry. And a cute new haircut that was more casual than conservative, more sporty than conventional.

She smiled at her reflection, noting the change in her. She was more relaxed, more in tune with her surroundings, more focused on her *life*, rather than her job. She felt like her life had slowed to a snail's pace compared to the constant movement that she had been in. There was nothing slow-paced about Chicago, and her job had reflected that as well. Everyone was in a hurry, yet everybody seemed to be behind schedule in whatever they did. Her included. There never seemed to be a time where she could simply stop and breathe.

Here? It was so very different. Despite the tragic reason she was here, despite the fact that her parents weren't quite back to normal yet—would they ever be?—she was embracing her time in Rockport. She felt...free. She felt like the constraints she'd had on her, constraints she'd mostly placed on herself, were now gone. Did she dare say she was almost a different person?

So much so that she trusted a twenty-three-year-old guy to close up Fat Larry's after only one day of training. The control she insisted on having in her job, in her life, had disappeared, it seemed.

A byproduct of Matt's death? Perhaps. Or maybe it was just being away from her real life, her real responsibilities, the constant stress she lived with. Maybe removing herself from that, even if only for a little while, had changed her.

Regardless, she wanted to embrace it. Because it felt good.

So with a smile on her face, she dressed in soft cotton athletic shorts and slipped her feet into flip-flops—a cheap pair she'd snagged at the local Walmart. Feeling relaxed and casual, she decided to skip her bra and slipped a navy-colored Fat Larry T-shirt over her head.

She found Annie in the kitchen, cutting up potatoes. She was surprised—and pleased—that a bottle of wine was opened and a glass poured.

"Thanks," she said as she picked it up.

Annie glanced up at her and smiled, her gaze traveling slowly over her. Jordan felt a bit self-conscious without a bra. Her breasts were small, and though she doubted Annie would even know, she just barely resisted the urge to cross her arms over her chest.

"You're welcome." Her gaze returned to her face. "I love your hair like that. It's cute."

Jordan smiled and relaxed. "Thank you."

"Who did it?"

"Over at Quick Clips," she said. "I think her name was Laura."

Annie nodded as she went back to cutting the potatoes. "That's where I go too. Jasmine cuts mine."

Jordan shrugged. "It wasn't exactly planned. I made a run to the liquor store for wine."

Annie laughed. "It's right next door. What? Was it calling your name?"

"Something like that, yeah." Jordan walked closer, looking over her shoulder. "Need some help?"

"I'm about done. I just have to mix it all together. It has to bake for forty-five minutes."

"Okay. Then we've got lots of time before the chops need to go on."

"Take your wine out to the deck. I'll be there in a minute," Annie said. "Oh, and I bought me a bottle of sparkling apple cider, so you don't have to drink alone."

"I'll get it for you," she offered, finding it in the fridge.

She added a few ice cubes to a wineglass and filled it with the cider, then took both of them out to the deck. She turned the ceiling fan on and Annie joined her a few minutes later. She brought the wine bottle with her and she topped off Jordan's glass.

"It's so nice out here," Annie said, sitting down next to her near the railing. "Hard to believe it's mid-June already."

"There's always a breeze, it seems."

"I've noticed that you don't like to be inside much," Annie said. "Were you always like that?"

Jordan stared out over the bay. It hadn't really occurred to her, but yes, she'd spent very little time inside since she'd been back.

"I think it's because I was in the city so long," she said. "I live in a high-rise condo, I work in a high-rise office building.

I'm surrounded by steel and concrete, it seems." She turned her gaze to Annie. "I was thinking earlier how *free* I feel here, how relaxed I am. Everything has slowed down to a pace I can actually live with."

Annie nodded. "I can't imagine living in a big city. Not anymore, anyway. When I was in high school, I used to fantasize about living in New York or Los Angeles," she said. "Even when I was married and…well, hating it, I used to think about running away to a city somewhere."

"But now?"

"I'm content," Annie said. "I love the slow pace. What I used to think was so boring, now is…well, it's familiar. It's home."

Jordan nodded but didn't comment. She felt Annie watching her and she turned, meeting her gaze.

"Why did you leave and not come back?"

"That's easy," Jordan said. "Because I was gay and I was terrified of my family finding out. I massed together a bunch of scholarships and headed to California for college. Berkley. I had a great time," she said with a smile. But that smile left her face. "Until my parents and Matt came over for a surprise visit."

"Oh, no."

Jordan smiled again. "Oh, yeah. Let's just say they were a lot more surprised than I was."

"So they found out, huh?"

"Yeah. And my mother's tears convinced me that they hated me. So I withdrew from them even more. Got a job in Chicago. Worked my ass off, seventy hours a week. Made a lot of money, moved up in the company…" She shrugged but said no more.

"And?"

"And nothing. That's it."

"But your family…Matt…"

"Oh, I learned that they really did love me," she said. "But I was entrenched in my job there, my…my life. I didn't make it back here very often."

Annie stared at her. "You feel guilty?" she asked gently.

Jordan nodded. "Yes. It's been years since I've been here, years since I saw Matt. I missed out on so much. I hadn't even talked to him on the phone in months," she said. She turned, looking back over the shimmering water of the bay, the approaching sunset casting an orange glow. "I miss him."

Jordan was surprised when she felt a soft hand touch her forearm. She turned, feeling Annie's fingers slide along her arm, ending with their fingers entwined. It felt…nice. Jordan met her gaze, those blue-green eyes shadowed.

"What is it?" she nearly whispered.

Annie visibly swallowed. "I…I have to tell you something."

Jordan nodded. "Okay."

"Matt," Annie said quietly. "Matt…is the father."

Their eyes were locked together, Jordan shocked by her words. Her brother was the father of Annie's baby? That, she had never considered.

"I'm sorry," Annie said. "I didn't know how to tell you."

"But…you said you and Matt…that you weren't—"

"I know. And we weren't," Annie said. She squeezed Jordan's fingers, then released them. "I'm…I'm not even sure how it happened." She rolled her eyes. "Well, obviously, I know how it happened, but the circumstances…God, it's just all so crazy," she said.

"You weren't dating?"

Annie shook her head. "No. And don't get me wrong, Matt was a super nice guy. I'd known him all through school," she said. "And he flirted with me, like he always did. I just wasn't attracted to him."

Jordan frowned. "Then why?"

"Why?" Annie looked away, her turn to stare out over the bay. "It was a rainy, stormy night and I was lonely. I thought I had…issues," she said. "And I didn't want to have *issues*."

"Issues?"

Annie glanced back at her but shook her head. "Nothing. I just…I hadn't been with anyone since I divorced Derrick. I had no interest, really. I went out with a few guys, but…there was nothing there. And Matt…he flirted with me, teased me." She drank the last of her cider. "That night, I thought…what the hell? We closed the store together. It was just the two of us."

She covered her face with her hands. "I should have stopped it. Matt was only a friend." She uncovered her face and looked at Jordan. "When I didn't feel anything, I should have stopped it."

"But you slept with him anyway."

Annie nodded. "On the sofa in his office."

"Eww," Jordan said. "The *same* sofa?"

"Yes."

Jordan shook her head. "The first thing I'm doing is getting rid of that sofa."

Annie smiled. "Thank you. I'd like it if you did."

Jordan leaned forward, resting her elbows on her knees. "So? You slept together. Then what?"

Annie let out her breath. "It was...it was awful. I started crying and he started apologizing, and it was very, very awkward." She again reached out and took Jordan's hand. "We left the store, and he said he was going to Port Aransas. It was storming. He shouldn't have been out."

Jordan squeezed her fingers. "Oh, my God. That was the night he died."

"Yes. And I kept thinking, did he go to Port A because of me? Because of what happened? I mean—"

"You can't blame yourself, Annie. That's crazy."

"Is it?" Annie wiped a tear from her cheek. "What if I hadn't freaked out? What if I hadn't slept with him in the first place? Would he still be alive?"

"Stop it. There's no blame here, Annie."

Jordan refilled her wineglass with a shaking hand. Annie was pregnant with Matt's baby. Wow. She didn't see that coming.

"I should have told you earlier," Annie said.

Jordan glanced back at her. "It's okay."

"Is it?"

Jordan gave her a smile. "Yeah. It's...okay."

Annie looked away from her. "Your parents are going to hate me."

Jordan laughed. "Quite the opposite, I'd think."

Annie turned to her again. "Really?"

"They'll love that a part of Matt is still with us. They'll love that, Annie."

Jordan was surprised that her words brought tears to Annie's eyes. She would have hoped they would have brought relief instead. She stood quickly, drawing Annie to her feet. She pulled her into a tight hug, feeling Annie's arms slip around her waist as she clung to her.

"It'll all be okay," she said as she lightly rubbed Annie's back.

"I'm so sorry," Annie murmured against her chest.

"It's okay."

Annie pulled back a little, meeting her eyes. "Will you be with me when I tell your parents?"

Jordan nodded. "Of course."

CHAPTER SIXTEEN

Annie mindlessly folded another T-shirt and placed it in the proper bin. It was a chore she no longer had to do since having been promoted to office manager, but she found she missed it. The monotony of it allowed her mind to wander aimlessly, and this morning she was focused on her upcoming meeting with Jordan's parents. She still had three more days. Jordan had invited them over for dinner on Sunday. Annie had told her she would be too nervous to cook anything so Jordan was going the simple route—steak and baked potatoes.

"Do you want me to finish that?"

Annie looked up to find Molly watching her. The T-shirt she'd been folding was still clutched in her hand. Apparently, she couldn't let her mind wander and still work after all.

"Yes, thanks," Annie said, handing her the shirt. "I should get started on the inventory before Jordan gets here."

Molly had the shirt folded before Annie could even turn away. Molly was a good hire. She was sharp as a tack and willing to do anything. After only three weeks, she was already running circles around Jessica. She was also the complete opposite of Jessica. Matt hired based on looks. Everyone knew that. Jordan, however, was more interested in brains. The two high school students she'd hired—Molly and Steven—were both in the top part of their class. Molly lacked Jessica's long blond hair and good looks, but she was a quick learner and needed no supervision. And Steven, while looking every bit the nerd that he was, had already helped Jordan set up a new inventory system that could link directly to QuickBooks and their accounts.

And to think both of them had only been there three weeks. She glanced over to where Jessica was. She was bobbing her head to the music as she restocked the coffee mugs. Annie could tell from here that she already had them out of order. Oh well. Molly would straighten them out later.

It was still ten minutes until the store opened, so she went to the back for another cup of coffee. Decaf. While her doctor had recommended that she limit her caffeine intake to one cup of coffee per day, Annie was a three- or four-cup-a-day drinker. She'd adhered to the one-cup rule on Monday and thought she'd made it through with flying colors. Apparently, Jordan thought otherwise. Tuesday morning, Jordan had brought out a Keurig and an assortment of decaf pods for her to choose from.

"What are you trying to say?" she'd asked Jordan.

"That you were a little cranky yesterday."

"I was not."

"You nearly made Jessica cry. And you snapped at me over the color choice for the new Fat Larry T-shirts."

Well, yeah, there was that, she conceded. So on Tuesday, she had four cups of decaf. And a splitting headache. So yesterday, she'd had one cup of *real* coffee, then finished up with decaf. No headache.

"So I'm an addict," she murmured as the coffee dripped into her cup.

"Who are you talking to?"

Annie turned, finding Jordan leaning against the office door. "What are you doing here? I thought you were coming in at noon."

"Got here a little while ago," Jordan said. "How's the headache?"

Annie smiled. "None today. I had my caffeine fix earlier," she said. "You want a cup?"

Jordan shook her head. "I've already got one, thanks."

She went back into the office and Annie followed. She stopped and stared at the empty space. She looked over at Jordan.

"When did you move the sofa?"

"Had a couple of guys come get it. They just left."

"I guess they were quiet. I didn't hear a thing." She took a sip of her coffee. "New one?"

"Yes. On the way."

Annie was glad to be rid of the old one. While she didn't mind the memories of Matt, she didn't like that her mind went immediately to *that night* each and every time she looked at it.

"Thank you," she said.

"Well, I did promise I'd get rid of it," Jordan said. "You weren't the only one having visions when you looked at it, you know."

Annie felt her face turn to what she assumed was a bright red. "You did *not* just say that!"

Jordan laughed. "What?"

Annie shook her head. "Can we rearrange the office while we're at it? Turn it into something completely different?"

"Sure. Whatever you want."

So before the guys came with the new sofa, she and Jordan moved the desk against the side wall where they would now have a view of the door leading into the store. The bookshelf was moved to where the sofa used to be. She vacuumed while Jordan hooked up the printer again.

When they came with the new sofa, Annie got out of the way and let Jordan guide them inside. It was a smaller sofa and much nicer than the old one. While the old one was a drab beige cloth, this one was smooth dark leather. She couldn't wait to sit on it. The guys made quick work of it and Jordan tipped them both before closing the back delivery door behind them.

"Well?" Jordan asked.

Annie sank down on the sofa and nodded. "Nice. Really nice," she said as she ran her hands across the cool leather. "It makes it look like a real office now."

"Good. I thought you'd like it," Jordan said.

Annie got up again. "I do. Thank you." She walked over to her and touched Jordan's arm, letting her fingers linger on her skin. "You didn't have to do that, you know."

"Trust me. I did," Jordan said with a smile.

Annie was aware of their closeness and knew she should move, knew she should remove her hand from Jordan's arm. But she didn't. Her fingers tightened of their own will as she met Jordan's eyes. How many seconds she stood there, she didn't know. Long enough. But when the back door opened, she took a quick, guilty step away, separating them. She was surprised by the slight blush on Jordan's face.

"Just a head's up," Jessica said. "A church bus stopped out front."

Jordan frowned. "What? Are they going to protest or something?"

Annie laughed. "I think she meant to warn us that we're going to be overrun with customers soon." She patted Jordan's arm as she walked past, heading out to help Jessica and Molly with the crowd.

* * *

Jordan let out her breath when Annie left. Unconsciously, she touched her arm where Annie's fingers had been.

"What just happened?" she whispered.

Okay, yeah, Annie liked to touch. She'd learned that weeks ago. But since when did *she* like to be touched?

She shook that thought away and sat down at the desk, pulling the laptop closer. Thursday was the day they did inventory and placed orders for the next week. Matt had normally placed orders once a month, but Annie had convinced her to do it weekly for T-shirts. That way, they would know which ones were good sellers and which were not. No sense in having their inventory stocked with shirts no one was buying.

Their normal Thursday routine had Jordan coming in at noon. Annie would have already finished the inventory, thanks to Steven and the new system he'd built for them. Jordan would then decide on quantity and place the orders.

She'd thrown a kink into that today by arriving early. Truth was, it was a rather hot day and instead of being outside, she had decided to head to the store. Well, that was sort of the truth. It was quiet and lonely at the house, and she found herself staring out at the bay with no desire or motivation to do anything, even though the lawn needed to be mowed. She'd also talked to her father about having a new pier built. When they came out on Sunday, he was going to take a look at it. She had offered to split the expense with him, but she doubted he would take her up on the offer.

She looked up as the door opened. She liked this new setup of the office. The desk had a view of the open area and the door. It was Annie.

"The church group didn't stay long," she said. "Thankfully. It was mostly kids, and they managed to make a complete mess of the T-shirts."

"Good thing it was too early for popcorn," she said.

Annie leaned her shoulder against the doorframe. "Are you managing inventory or do you need me to help?"

Jordan could have managed just fine. But she'd rather have Annie's company. She got up and pointed to the laptop.

"Do your thing."

Annie smiled as she walked past her. "My *thing*?"

Jordan returned her smile. "Well, you do your thing better than I do."

Annie's laugh was nearly contagious. "I'm not going to touch that statement."

CHAPTER SEVENTEEN

Annie paced nervously in the living room, back and forth across the rug. They would be arriving any minute, she knew, and she wasn't really prepared.

"Relax."

She looked up, finding Jordan watching her. She shook her head. "I can't. I'm nervous."

Jordan came closer. "They'll be shocked. Then they'll be excited."

"You don't know that. They could hate me. They could—"

"Annie, they're not going to hate you."

Annie plunged her hands into her hair. "I'm not ready. I'm not—"

"It'll be fine."

Annie's "easy for you to say" reply was stuck in her throat. Jordan had taken her hands and linked their fingers, holding Annie's arms to her side. They were standing only inches apart, and Annie was having a hard time catching her breath.

"Look at me."

Annie blinked several times, trying to focus on Jordan's gaze.

"We're going to have a nice, casual dinner. They're going to get to know you better. They'll love you, Annie. How could they not?"

Annie tilted her head. "Do we *have* to tell them?"

Jordan laughed, then pulled her into a tight hug. Annie sank against her, loving her strength, loving the security she felt in her arms. But something else was just below the surface, just out of reach. She closed her eyes, trying to find it, but it eluded her. Instead, gentle hands rubbed her back, and she let out a contented sigh. She could have stayed there for hours, but Jordan loosened her hold and Annie took that as her cue to take a step away from her.

"So? You okay?"

Annie nodded. "I guess."

"Good. Because I think they're here."

Annie's heart beat nervously as Jordan went to the door to greet her parents. Annie had met them before, of course, but it was always at the store and their conversations had been short and polite, nothing more than a greeting really. Now, here she was about to have dinner with them, about to tell them that she was carrying Matt's baby.

"Oh, dear God," she murmured. But then, it couldn't be any worse than her own parents' reaction. And she had survived that. So she plastered a smile on her face and waited while Jordan greeted them both with hugs and a kiss on the cheek.

"You know Annie, of course," Jordan said.

"Yes, of course. How are you, dear?"

Annie greeted Jordan's mother with a smile and then a quick handshake with her father. "I'm good, thanks," she said, hoping the words sounded a little less formal to them than they did to her own ears.

"How do you like living out here on the bay?" Jordan's father asked.

"Oh, I love it. Jordan was a lifesaver," she said, taking a quick glance at Jordan, who smiled back at her.

Jordan's mother took her arm and led her into the kitchen, and she looked over her shoulder, hoping Jordan would join them. Instead, Jordan and her father headed out to the deck.

"I heard about...well, about your mother not taking the news too well."

Annie stared at her. "News?"

"About you being pregnant. I try to put myself in her shoes, but you just can't deny your children, no matter what. I'm glad that Jordan offered the spare room to you."

"Thank you. My mother, well, she's not quite ready to accept it yet. I've found the less we talk, the less we argue."

"She shouldn't miss out on this. You look beautiful, Annie. I'd even say glowing."

Annie blushed. "Mrs. Sims, I don't know that I'd say glowing, but at least the morning sickness has subsided somewhat."

She laughed. "You will call me Loraine. None of that Mrs. Sims nonsense," she said with a wave of her hand. "And David goes by Dave to his friends."

"Thank you." Annie couldn't believe how totally at ease she felt around her. Of course, once she told Loraine who the father was, that all could change.

"Now, I know Jordan," Loraine continued as they stood in the large kitchen. "She'll have steaks and baked potatoes and nothing else."

Annie laughed. "Yes, you do know her. But I did pick up some vegetables to steam. I hope that will be enough."

"Oh, good. I meant to bring the fixings for a salad but completely forgot," she said. She went to the fridge and opened it. "It looks so different than when Matt lived here. Beer and a carton of milk were usually all you'd find."

The mention of Matt's name brought a nervous flutter to Annie's heart. Should she just blurt out the news?

But Loraine was sporting a smile, and Annie didn't want to chase it away. "I like to cook, so you can blame me," she said.

"Then I'll quit worrying that Jordan is eating takeout every night." She surprised Annie by taking two beers from the fridge.

"For Jordan and Dave," Loraine explained. "I can't stand the stuff."

"I drink sparkling apple cider when Jordan has wine," Annie said. "I will admit, I do miss having a glass of wine from time to time."

"Yes, I like wine too. Matt used to keep a stash here for me," Loraine said.

"I think Jordan has already gone through all that," Annie said with a laugh. "She thought it was Matt's stash, not yours."

"Oh, he would join me, but he was like Dave and preferred beer." Her smile faltered somewhat. "While I've finally accepted that he's gone, I sometimes miss him so much."

"I know. We miss him too," she said.

Loraine's smile was gentle. "You and Matt were…close?"

Annie nearly panicked. She knew what Loraine meant by that question, but she had no idea how to answer it. No, they weren't *close*, not like that. But yes, there was sex involved. Thankfully, she heard the back door open and she let out a relieved sigh when Jordan came in.

"Ah, just what I was looking for," Jordan said, taking the beer from her mother.

"Did you show him the pier?" Annie asked.

"Yep. And he agrees with me. He's going to have some guys come out to look at it next week."

"It needs repair?" Loraine asked.

"It needs replacing," Jordan said. "Why don't you come out on the deck? The breeze is nice."

"I think your mother would like a glass of wine," Annie said.

"Merlot?" Jordan asked.

"Whatever," Loraine said. "Something red."

Jordan handed the beer to her mother. "Here. Take that out to Dad. We'll be right out."

As soon as Loraine was out of earshot, Annie turned to Jordan. "Thank you. She was about to ask if Matt and I were dating," she said.

"How did that come up?" Jordan asked.

"We were just chatting," she said. "I like her. She said I should call her Loraine."

Jordan nodded as she turned the corkscrew. "Then that means she likes you."

Annie watched as Jordan pulled the cork out, then she went to the cabinet and took down two wineglasses, one for Loraine's wine and one for her cider. "Do you want me to bring the frozen mugs for your beer?"

"Just one for me. My dad likes the bottle."

They joined Jordan's parents out on the deck, and indeed, the breeze was nice. Annie didn't think they even needed the ceiling fan but Jordan put it on anyway.

"We used to come out here all the time when we were younger," Loraine said. "Well, when Jordan and Matt were young. Dave's parents were still alive then."

"Why did you stop coming?" Annie asked.

"Oh, I don't know. We just got so busy. And spare time was spent taking care of our home, we didn't make time for out here."

"That pier should have been replaced years ago," Dave said. "I wonder why Matt never said anything."

"You know how Matt was," Loraine said. "Jordan can attest to that. The house was a wreck."

"Housekeeping wasn't his strong suit," Jordan agreed.

"Had you been out here, Annie?" Loraine asked.

She nodded. "A couple of times," she said. "The last two summers, Matt would have an office party out here."

"Yeah, she's trying to talk me into having one too," Jordan said. "Annie thinks they might like me better if I do."

Loraine frowned. "Why don't they like you?"

Annie gave a quick laugh. "Because she has rules that Matt never did."

"Yeah, like showing up to work on time," Jordan said.

"So? Business has been good?" Dave asked.

Jordan shrugged. "I guess. Annie would know better than me. I'm not sure what summer crowds are supposed to be like."

Annie nodded. "Yes, it's been good." She turned to Jordan. "Which reminds me, we need to order some more Fat Larry T-shirts. Brandon said he gave out a lot of them yesterday."

"If we give out free T-shirts, doesn't that deter customers from buying them?" Loraine asked.

"Matt said it put them in a good mood and then they were more apt to buy something than not," Annie said. "Not sure if that was just his opinion or an actual marketing strategy," she added.

"It seems to work," Dave said. "I love seeing those T-shirts around town."

"We've got a new design," Jordan offered. "Fat Larry is still the same, of course, but with a new background."

Annie noticed the expression on Loraine's face and quickly added, "I think you'll love it. I know Matt would have."

Jordan gave her a nod and a subtle smile—a silent thank-you.

Loraine's expression softened a bit. "I know we said for you to run the store as you wanted," she said. "I just don't want to change up too much. Matt had everything running smoothly."

"I'm not changing stuff, Mom. A few tweaks here and there, that's all."

"She can handle it," Dave said. "I have to agree. Matt was a little lax sometimes with his employees. There has to be accountability. You know that from the restaurant."

Loraine nodded but didn't reply. There seemed to be a little tension in the air, and Annie assumed it was because they were discussing Matt as much as they were.

"I should get the steaks going," Jordan said. "Want another beer, Dad?"

"Thanks."

"Mom?"

"I'll take another glass of wine."

Annie stood quickly. "I'll get it."

She followed Jordan back inside, through the living room and into the kitchen. Their eyes met and Annie felt a little relief.

"I guess talking about Matt…"

"Yes, Mom still has her moments. But she's a lot better."

"Right before you came in earlier, she asked me if Matt and I were *close*," Annie said. "I nearly panicked. Should I lie? Should I tell her we were dating?"

"I don't think you have to lie, Annie."

"So I either lie to her or she thinks I'm a slut." She covered her face with her hands. "God, she's going to hate me."

She felt Jordan move closer, and she let her take her hands from her face.

"It'll be okay."

"You keep saying that. I'm not sure I believe you."

Jordan's fingers tightened around her own. "Trust me."

Annie nodded. "I will. But there's no easy way to tell them. Before dinner? During? After? Regardless of when, it'll still ruin dinner."

Jordan smiled at her. "Let's make it after dinner. Don't want to waste those expensive fillets."

CHAPTER EIGHTEEN

For all her brave words, Jordan was actually nervous. Of course, she knew Annie was as well. They'd had a nice dinner with pleasant conversation, and she and her mother had finished off the bottle of wine. She could tell by her father's demeanor that he was now ready to go home. She glanced over at Annie and raised her eyebrows. In return, Annie blew out a nervous breath and nodded. But before Annie could speak, Jordan decided to take the lead.

"Mom…Dad…there's something we need to tell you," she said. "Well, Annie…but still."

Her mother frowned and glanced between the two of them. "What's wrong?"

Annie stood up, twisting her hands together nervously. "There's no easy way," she said. "And I so wish there was."

"Okay, girls, you're scaring me," her mother said. "What is it?"

Annie looked over at her and Jordan nodded.

"As you know, I'm pregnant," Annie said. "What you don't know is that...Matt is the father."

Her mother's face turned ashen. "*What?*"

"I'm so sorry," Annie said immediately.

Jordan stood up. "Don't say you're sorry," she said. "It took two. It wasn't just you."

Her mother held both hands up. "Okay...stop. Now... *what?*"

Jordan walked in front of her mother. "Annie and Matt... were..."

"Dating?"

"Not exactly," Annie said.

"Then what?"

"Mom...let's don't go into details," Jordan said.

"Of course I want details," she said. "You're telling me that Matt fathered a child?"

"I know you'll want to do paternity tests and all," Annie said. "And that's fine. I just thought you should know."

Her mother leaned back in her chair. "You're pregnant with Matt's baby?"

Annie nodded. "Yes."

Her mother turned her gaze to Jordan. "And you knew?"

Jordan nodded. "Yes. She told me a few weeks ago."

Her mother looked back at Annie. "I had no idea that you two were involved. I mean, I'm glad to know that he had someone, but I wish he'd shared that with me."

Annie looked at her helplessly, and Jordan gave a slight shrug. Was it so bad to let her mother think that Matt had a love in his life?

Her father finally stirred and she recognized the shock on his face. Shock...and something else.

"Matt's baby?"

Annie simply nodded and that nod brought a smile to her father's face. "Wow," was all he said.

Her mother got up and went to Annie, wrapping her arms around her. Annie looked at Jordan over her mother's shoulder and Jordan saw the relieved look in her eyes. She smiled at her and Annie seemed to relax into her mother's hug.

"A baby," her mother said. "We're going to have a baby." She pulled away from Annie, her smile big. "That's wonderful news, dear. We, of course, will help you in any way you need."

"I'm glad you're living here with Jordan," her father said. He looked at her. "You're not charging her rent, are you?"

"No, Dad."

Annie held her hands up. "Look, I didn't tell you this because I wanted anything from you. I don't. But you deserved to know that Matt...well, that Matt—"

"Annie, it's only right that we support this child, that we support you," her mother said.

Jordan stepped forward. "Mom, let's give it time to sink in, okay. Right now, Annie is fine living here. And there's a lot of time to go."

"When are you due?" her mother asked.

"The end of January," Annie said.

"Matt was born in January." Tears gathered in her mother's eyes, and Annie was again engulfed in a hug. "That's wonderful." Then she pulled back and studied Annie. "You're not even showing yet."

Jordan watched as Annie's hand went to her abdomen. "My clothes are getting a little tight," she said.

"It'll happen soon enough."

Her mother then went over to her father and hugged him. "Isn't this wonderful news, Dave?"

"It sure is."

Annie glanced over at her with a smile, then took a step in her direction. Jordan walked closer too, letting their shoulders touch. Annie leaned into her.

"Thank you," she whispered.

"Told you," Jordan whispered back.

CHAPTER NINETEEN

"How do you want to work the festival?" Annie asked as soon as Jordan walked into the office.

Jordan raised her eyebrows. "What festival?"

"On the Fourth of July," she said. "Everyone will want to go."

Jordan sank down onto the sofa and took a sip from her coffee cup. "There's a festival?"

"Oh, Jordan, there's been a festival on the Fourth of July since we were kids. How can you not remember?"

Jordan shrugged. "I forgot a lot of stuff," she said. "So will we be busy here?"

"There'll be more people in town than normal, but most of them will be at the festival. We rent a booth there so we'll have to have someone work it too."

"We do?"

"I guess I didn't think to mention it to you. Matt always handled all of that," she said. "We take mostly T-shirts and a few things that are unbreakable."

"Okay. Well, that shouldn't be too hard, right?"

"We've got to have the store covered, the booth covered, and give them all an opportunity to go to the festival itself," she explained.

"What did you do last year?"

"Matt took the booth. Everyone else took short shifts here."

Jordan groaned. "I'm not crazy about the idea of working the booth."

Annie smiled at her. "Too many people for your liking?"

"If they all want to go to the festival, wouldn't it be easier to split the shifts at the booth?"

"And you'll work the store?"

"You and me?" Jordan asked hopefully.

Annie shook her head. Jordan still didn't like to be left at the store alone. What she was afraid of, Annie had no idea.

"How about we call a staff meeting and get their opinions?" Annie suggested.

"Okay. You're the manager. You call it." Jordan leaned forward, grabbing her reading glasses and the latest T-shirt catalog from the desk. "Have you looked at this yet?"

"Not really. I flipped through it is all," she said.

She pulled up the inventory, wondering if she should order more shirts before the festival. Certainly more of the Fat Larry T-shirts. Brandon was giving them away at a record pace. Matt would be proud. She glanced over at Jordan, watching her as she studied the catalog. She looked adorable with her reading glasses low on her nose.

"Do you know how cute you look in those glasses?" The words were out before Annie could stop them and she felt a slight blush on her face.

Jordan looked up, her eyes meeting Annie's over the top of her glasses. "Yeah. They make me look super-smart."

Annie leaned her elbows on the desk and rested her chin on her hands. "Why are you single?" When Jordan raised her eyebrows questioningly, Annie continued. "And don't say it's because you used to work sixty or seventy hours a week. That's just an excuse."

Jordan put the catalog down beside her on the sofa and tossed her glasses on top of it. "No, it's not really an excuse," Jordan said. "I had goals—professional goals—and priorities and my love life was never at the top of the list. It wasn't even *near* the top. And like a lot of things, the years kinda went by without me knowing it."

"So what's the longest relationship you've ever been in?"

Jordan laughed. "Does three dates constitute a relationship?"

"Oh, come on. Surely you've been out with someone more than three times."

Jordan leaned back on the sofa and crossed her legs, resting one ankle across her knee. "Well, there was Debra. We hung out for a while. Debra was an investment broker, so we had things in common. But she was very competitive, and it was always a power struggle with us." She grinned. "The sex was great."

"But?" Annie prompted.

Jordan shrugged. "We both knew it wasn't going anywhere. I think we were too much alike."

"Are you that competitive?"

Jordan nodded. "At work, yes." Before Annie could ask another question, Jordan asked one of her. "Why are *you* single?"

"Me?" Annie reached for her coffee cup, perhaps stalling for time. Why was she still single? "Well, the first time around was so disastrous, I was afraid to even consider dating again," she said. She looked over at Jordan, holding her gaze. "Truthfully, there never was anyone...well, I guess I learned from Derrick... our relationship was nothing more than high school *crap*," she said with a smile. "He was familiar, he was who my parents loved, our friends were all getting married, so I simply followed suit. But I never...I never felt for Derrick what you need for a marriage. I knew that. I knew that six months after we got married. I probably knew it before we got married."

"You've been divorced...what? Four years or so?"

"Yes. I guess I just haven't met anyone who...well, who..." She stared at Jordan, feeling a connection with her that she couldn't quite understand. Jordan's eyes were gentle and Annie didn't want to pull away. "Maybe...someday," she said quietly.

Jordan nodded. "Yeah. Me too."

Annie smiled and finally pulled her gaze away. "I guess I should get back to my inventory."

Jordan stood. "I'll go cover the store if you want to get a vote on the festival."

"Okay, thanks. Jessica and Staci aren't working today, but I'll get their take tomorrow," Annie said.

Jordan paused at the door. "I've also been thinking about this office party you want me to have."

"Oh, yeah?"

"Mid-July work for you?"

"Sure. I don't know that I'll fit into a swimsuit by then, though," she said. "My clothes are starting to get a little tight."

"You can't tell."

"When I'm naked looking in the mirror, I can tell," she said.

A smile touched Jordan's face and she looked like she wanted to say something but didn't. Annie smiled too.

"Whatever it is you're thinking…"

Jordan laughed. "Not going to say." She took a step back into the office. "But when will you tell the others?"

"I don't know. Part of me wants to wait until it's obvious. Maybe they'll just think I'm getting fat," she said.

"Think you'll be embarrassed by what they think?"

"Yes. Especially when they find out it's Matt's," she said. "They'll assume we were having this clandestine affair right under their noses."

Jordan shrugged. "Doesn't matter, does it?"

Annie sighed. "Staci had a little crush on him. She used to tease that I did too."

"Ah. So she'll think you were lying to her."

"Yes." Annie waved a hand at Jordan. "I don't do drama well. And I feel there's going to be drama." She leaned back in her chair and stared at the ceiling. "And when Derrick finds out, he's going to totally freak out." She looked at Jordan. "Please promise me you won't let him back here. Because he'll try to storm back here and confront me."

"I promise I'll protect you."

"Thank you."

Jordan turned to go but again paused and turned back. "By the way, if we can both sneak out of here early today, I thought maybe we could take a Jet Ski ride out in the bay."

"Really?" Annie grinned. "That would be fun."

"They're going to start on the pier in a couple of days. I need to move them anyway."

"Okay. I'm game."

Jordan nodded. "Good. I'll pick up dinner at the restaurant."

Annie was still smiling long after Jordan left. A Jet Ski ride in the bay? She could hardly wait.

CHAPTER TWENTY

Jordan pulled the Jet Ski closer to the shore where Annie stood. She tried not to stare, but Annie's bikini top was too revealing. It was also the first time she'd seen Annie in one.

"I know. My breasts are *huge* already," Annie said.

Jordan laughed. "They are not."

Annie actually cupped herself, and Jordan was surprised by the blush that caused.

"I've always been teased because of my small breasts," Annie said. "So they are *huge* to me."

Jordan pointed at herself. "This is small. When I was growing up, I was terrified I would never get breasts. Gym class was not fun," she said, remembering the teasing from the other girls.

"I know. I hated it too."

Jordan lifted the seat and pulled out two lifejackets, handing one to Annie. Those "huge" breasts were soon covered. She slipped on her own and tightened the straps.

"All set," Annie said.

Jordan steadied the Jet Ski, then held her hand out to Annie. "Climb on then."

Annie gripped Jordan around the waist, then loosened her hold, resting her hands on Jordan's sides lightly. Jordan acknowledged that it had been a very long time since she'd been this close to another woman. But…this was Annie. It shouldn't feel this good.

"Ready?"

"Yep."

Jordan was conscious of the hands that squeezed tightly as she sped away from shore. Well, "sped" was stretching the truth. As she'd told Annie, it had been years since she'd been on a Jet Ski. During the summer months, she and Matt had been on them all the time. But once she left for college—and stayed away as much as she did—her love of speeding across the bay at breakneck speeds vanished. Or maybe it was just that she got older. She did, however, enjoy a boat ride from time to time on her visits. She was sorry that her father had sold the boat. She would much rather be cruising the barrier islands in a boat now than playing on Jet Skis.

The water was calm, and she dared to increase her speed a little. Annie's hands tightened again as she sped up, then relaxed against her.

"I've lived here my whole life and I still don't know the shrimping schedule," Annie said. "There are no boats out."

"Early mornings before dawn, I think," she said.

Annie leaned closer. "If you're worried about me, don't be. You can go faster if you want."

Jordan turned her head, finding Annie's face only inches from her own. "I did promise I wouldn't dump you," she reminded her. "I'm not that experienced anymore."

But she accelerated slightly, enjoying the breeze as it ruffled her hair. She stayed close to shore and did not venture out into the open water of the bay. They cruised along the north shore and she slowed from time to time, pointing out certain things to Annie that she remembered from her childhood. When they reached the east shore near the causeway, she turned around instead of going under it. Maybe another time they could go under it and go explore along the state park there to the south. Even though they had a nice view of the sunset from their deck, she remembered a spot at the park where they used to go with her grandparents. The entire bay seemed to be on fire as the sun set.

They encountered a fishing boat on the way back. Judging by the gulls following it, its crew was having success. The waves it created stirred the bay and Jordan had a little fun as they bounced over each one, causing Annie to laugh with delight.

As they returned to their own rickety pier, true to its name, four white pelicans were resting on the boards and another was coming in for a landing. Jordan slowed to a crawl so as not to disturb them.

"Oh, that was fun," Annie said. "We should do that more often."

"Yeah, it was. We'll do it again," she said.

The pelicans never moved as she crept closer. Instead of docking where Matt had kept the Jet Skis, she grounded it near the shore. The pier would be coming down in the next few days. She held the craft steady as Annie climbed off, then she swung her leg over the side and secured the Jet Ski between two pillars closer to shore. She kept the line taut enough so that during high tide it wouldn't drift and slam into the concrete retaining wall. Once the new pier was in place, she'd replace the old bumper tires with new ones and keep the Jet Ski in a little deeper water, like Matt had done.

"You want to eat on the deck?"

Jordan got out of the water and walked up beside Annie as they headed to the house. "Do you mind?"

"Of course not. It's pleasant out. Maybe because I'm a little wet."

"There's a place over by the state park," she said, giving voice to her earlier thoughts. "We used to go out there to catch the sunset and have a late picnic. The causeway makes for a great background."

Annie smiled at her. "Does that mean you want to go?"

"Maybe we'll plan a trip for another day. We used to take the boat. I don't know that'd I want to stay out that late on the Jet Ski though. It's a long way back here."

Annie nudged her. "You know, we could always *drive* over there."

Jordan laughed. "I suppose we could, but it'd take all the adventure out of it."

They each went into their separate bedrooms to change out of swimsuits and into shorts. Jordan loved the soft cotton fabric of her old gray athletic shorts and she rummaged in her drawer for a tank top. She picked up a bra, then tossed it down again. Since they'd already discussed breast sizes, she didn't see the point of trying to hide them.

Feeling cool and comfortable, she grabbed a beer from the fridge and turned off the oven. She'd picked up fish and shrimp and two containers of gumbo from the restaurant and had left the oven on warm while they were out.

"What some cider?" she called.

"Please."

It was still early and Jordan thought their dinner could wait a few minutes longer. She pulled two chairs closer to the deck railing where they could watch the changing colors as dusk approached. The low line of clouds shimmered in orange and red, almost like a stroke of a painter's brush across canvas.

She turned when Annie came out, then quickly averted her eyes. Annie, too, had apparently decided a bra was too much this evening. Her white Fat Larry T-shirt was not quite as loose on her as before.

"Are you starving or can we wait a bit?"

"I'm fine," Annie said as she sat down beside her. "Thanks," she said, indicating the apple cider.

"So what did you decide to do about the festival?"

"You were right. They all thought splitting shifts at the booth made more sense. Except for Molly. She said she'd rather work the store. In fact, she volunteered to work all day."

"What's up with that?"

Annie shrugged. "I think she's...well, a little awkward. Socially, I mean," Annie said.

"She seems fine with customers."

"Oh, I know. I meant with her peers. I'm only guessing, but I'd imagine she gets teased in school."

"Teased? Why?"

"Come on, Jordan. She's plain Jane. She's nearly at the top of her class. She doesn't dress in the most fashionable of clothes." Annie glanced at her. "Even Jessica kinda picks on her."

"I don't like Jessica very much."

Annie laughed. "You don't say?"

"Compared to Molly, Jessica is as dumb as a box of rocks," she said.

"She's also very attractive."

"If you say so."

"You don't think so?"

Jordan shook her head. "She's not really my type." As soon as she said that, she knew what Annie's next question would be.

Annie turned in her chair. "And?"

"And?"

"And…what is your type?"

Jordan considered the question for a moment. Did she even have a type? As an adult, most of her dates had been with professional women. Like Debra. But was that really her type? When she'd been in college and first exploring her sexuality, she tended to gravitate toward the sporty, athletic type. But maybe that was just a byproduct of who her friends were and the fact that she played intramural sports.

"Maybe it's not so much looks that define my type," she finally said. "I think I prefer someone who is…real."

"Real?"

"Yeah. Real. Honest. True. No agendas, no pretenses." She looked at Annie. "Genuine. And people like Jessica fit none of those."

Annie met her gaze, holding it. "And when you were dating before—Debra—did any of those descriptions fit her?"

Jordan smiled slightly. "Not really, no."

Annie nodded. "Makes sense then that you ended things with her."

Jordan arched an eyebrow. "Maybe she ended things with me."

"She would be crazy."

Jordan raised both eyebrows and Annie blushed slightly.

"I mean…you're attractive, you're nice. And you already said the sex was great."

"Well, thank you for thinking I'm nice," she said. Then she smiled. "*And* attractive."

Annie laughed. "Oh, stop pretending you don't know how cute you are."

Jordan was usually indifferent to her looks, but for some reason, it pleased her that Annie thought she was attractive. She thought Annie was as well. Her blond hair was just dark enough to be natural and her blue-green eyes were warm and inviting. When she realized those very eyes were looking back at her, she blinked her thoughts away.

"How about dinner?"

* * *

Annie rubbed her belly and nearly groaned. She shouldn't have had that last piece of fish. Or the last two shrimp. And she probably shouldn't have requested seconds on the gumbo.

"I'm going to be as big as a house," she said. "You've got to stop bringing home food from your parents' restaurant."

"I know. But it's so easy."

"Tomorrow night I'll cook. Something healthy," she said as she helped Jordan clear the table. It occurred to her how presumptuous she was being to assume they would have dinner together. But then again, not really. They shared dinner together most evenings. In fact, it was rare if they didn't.

"How about something vegetarian?" Jordan suggested.

"God, not that healthy," she said with a smile.

"How much weight have you gained?"

Annie stared at her. "Why? Can you tell I'm getting fat?"

"You're not getting fat. It was an innocent question," Jordan said.

Annie lifted up her shirt, exposing her belly. "Look. I can't button my shorts any longer."

Jordan surprised her by reaching out and touching her stomach and patting it lightly before taking her hand away. The touch was so unexpected she forgot to breathe.

"Yeah, that baby bump is starting to show."

Annie grabbed her arm tightly. "Do you really think so? Is it time to tell people?"

"You'll be three months along pretty soon, right?"

"Another two weeks, yes."

So far, she'd only told Suzanne and Macy. And her parents, of course. The only others who knew were Jordan and her parents. She had hoped to keep it a secret for as long as she could. But then, why? Was she embarrassed by it? Well, to some extent, yes. She never once thought that she'd be an unwed mother. The truth was, once she got divorced, she had given little thought to ever having kids. Yet here she was, nearly three months pregnant.

"I'm scared," she said. She felt tears in her eyes and wiped them away. "Damn my hormones," she murmured.

Jordan pulled her into a hug, and Annie slipped her arms around Jordan's waist as she pressed against her.

"I know you're scared," Jordan said. "But you don't have to be."

"My mother barely speaks to me," she said. "She hasn't invited me over once since I left."

"So go see her. Or better yet, let's invite them over here for dinner."

Annie pulled back a little and met her gaze. "Why would you want to do that?"

Jordan smiled. "They can't be that bad. They need to see you, Annie. To see how beautiful you look. To know that you're okay. To know that it's...real."

Annie stared into Jordan's dark eyes. "You think I'm beautiful?"

Jordan pulled her close again. "Yes, I think you're absolutely beautiful."

Annie closed her eyes, feeling safe and protected. "You don't think I'm fat?"

Jordan laughed. "Are you going to ask me that every day?"

Annie finally realized how intimate their embrace was, and she untangled herself from Jordan. "Thank you."

"You're welcome."

Annie let out her breath. "I'm tired. I think I'm going to shower and go to bed early."

"Okay. I'm going to watch a little TV, I guess. Will that disturb you?"

"No, that's fine."

She turned to go, then stopped. She leaned closer to Jordan, kissing her lightly on her cheek. "Thank you for everything, Jordan. I mean that sincerely."

Jordan simply nodded but didn't say anything. The look on her face said that she was surprised by Annie's impromptu kiss.

Annie was surprised as well.

CHAPTER TWENTY-ONE

Jordan stood at the back door, looking out over the mostly empty store. Annie and Molly were in the center checkout area, chatting. There were only two customers. Even though Annie had told her it would be slow, she still assumed that with this many people in town for the festival, they would be busy.

Yesterday evening, she and Annie had helped Brandon and Steven set up the booth. Brandon had been in charge of the inventory, and he'd come by the store first thing this morning to pick up the T-shirts he'd chosen. Ever since she'd given him the responsibility of closing, Brandon had become much more enthused about his job. Even though he'd always been cordial and friendly, he had much more of an "I care" attitude about him now. If she and Annie were both gone from the store, she had no qualms about putting him in charge.

The bell chimed on the front door, and she absently watched the two customers leave. It was only eleven and the morning had already been endless.

"You bored?"

She smiled and nodded, then joined Annie and Molly. "Seriously, why are we even open today?"

Annie shrugged. "Most all the shops stay open."

"Do they also have booths at the festival?"

"Some do."

Jordan looked out the windows to the empty street. Well, empty of foot traffic. Plenty of cars were driving past. Unfortunately they weren't stopping. They were heading down to the city park where the festival was going on.

"I say at noon we put a sign on the door telling people if they want a T-shirt to find our booth at the festival."

"I don't mind staying here," Molly said. "I wasn't planning on going to the festival anyway."

Jordan glanced briefly at Annie, remembering their discussion about Molly from the other night.

"Why don't you go?" she asked. "I thought it was a big deal."

Molly fidgeted with the keychain display, rearranging the rings by color. "Just hordes of people there," she said. "Same thing every year. Same booths, same food, same music."

"When I was in high school, we'd have a group of friends that would go," Annie said. "It was fun."

Molly shrugged.

"You know, if you don't have anyone to go with, you can hang with me and Annie," Jordan offered. Then she glanced at Annie. "Unless you're going with someone else."

Annie smiled. "I would love to go with you." She turned to Molly. "How about it?"

Molly looked at them skeptically. "What will we do?"

"Well I, for one, want a corn dog and some funnel cake," Annie said. "Or maybe a turkey leg."

Jordan laughed. "I'm not surprised your wish list involves food."

Annie pretended to be shocked by her statement. "And what exactly is it that you're trying to say?"

"Nothing. I love a woman who likes to eat," she said easily. "I'm going to go work on that sign for the door. Why don't you call Brandon and see if they need anything for the booth?" she suggested.

"Okay. Surely they're doing a better business than we are."

* * *

Annie walked between Jordan and Molly. She wasn't certain which of them looked more uncomfortable. She knew Jordan didn't like "hordes of people," as Molly had described the festival, but she looked nearly terrified as they fought through the crowd.

She bumped Jordan's shoulder lightly. "You okay?"

"Let's just say, I'd rather be sitting on our deck drinking a cold beer."

"Does that mean you want to head to the beer tent?"

"Let's hit the food booths first."

Annie again bumped her shoulder. "Thank you."

Jordan laughed but said nothing.

Annie turned to Molly. "Are any of your friends here?"

"Pretty much everybody at school goes," she said.

Annie took that to mean that she didn't really have any close friends. She felt sorry for her. She really liked Molly. She was smart and efficient, but she was also a pleasure to talk to. She had none of the adolescent quirks that Jessica still harbored. But she didn't want to embarrass Molly, so she said nothing else about would-be friends.

They stopped at the first food booth they came to and Annie looked over the menu. It was mostly barbeque and burgers, two things she was not in the mood for. She shook her head at Jordan's unasked question and they moved on.

"I see corn dogs," Molly said, pointing to a booth.

"Jackpot," Annie said. Without thinking, she linked arms with Jordan and pulled her toward the booth. "Do you like them?"

"I couldn't tell you the last time I had one."

"But you're game?"

"Sure. I'll try it."

When Jordan fished out money from her pocket, Annie pushed it away. "My treat. Molly? You want one too?"

"Okay."

They soon had three fat corn dogs covered in mustard, hers more than Molly's or Jordan's. She moaned when she took the first bite. Of all things to crave…corn dogs?

"Pretty good," Jordan said.

Annie nodded. "Okay, this will hold me for a little while. We can hit the beer tent now."

"Do you know the bands that are playing?" Jordan asked.

Annie shook her head. "Molly? Do you?"

"One is country music, but I don't know the other one," she said.

"Do you have an interest in listening?" Annie asked her.

"If you want to," Molly said. "I'm only tagging along."

"Jordan?"

Jordan shrugged. "Sure." She looked around. "Shouldn't we at least pop over to our booth, though?"

"Let's get something to drink first," she said. "And if we pass a booth with turkey legs, let me know."

They had no luck with turkey legs, but she did manage to snag a funnel cake along the way. Brandon and Staci were at the booth, and she was happy to see they at least had customers. The new design they had on the Fat Larry T-shirts was apparently a good seller, even though at the store Brandon gave them away in record numbers.

"Busy?" Jordan asked.

"Yeah, it's been good," Brandon said. "I take it the store was not."

"We made maybe five sales all morning," Jordan said.

"Do you need me to work?" Molly offered.

"Jessica is supposed to come at two," he said. "Staci just got here. I was about to take a break."

"We can hang around if you want," Jordan said.

"I think Molly and Staci can handle it," Annie countered, seeing the relieved look on Molly's face.

Jordan apparently saw it too. "Okay. Well, let's go walk around then. Maybe we'll run into a turkey leg."

For the next hour, they mingled with the crowd, going from booth to booth. There were a lot of homemade crafts, some local artists selling their paintings, local photographers with prints and several booths offering handcrafted pottery. But it was a display of wood carvings that drew her.

"Come look at this," she said. "We could carry some of these in the store."

Jordan picked up a small carving of a pelican and raised her eyebrows. "Not at this price," she said, showing it to Annie.

"Wow," Annie whispered.

They moved on, walking in communal silence, commenting from time to time on the different displays. They soon found themselves at the edge of the festival and near the marina.

"Feel like going?" Jordan asked, motioning to the water. "I haven't been down here in forever."

"Sure."

"When my parents first opened the restaurant, we used to come down here all the time to buy shrimp off the boats," Jordan said.

"And fish?"

"They'd get their fish from Al's, down in Fulton. I think they still do," she said.

"If they had the restaurant, why Fat Larry's?"

Jordan shook her head. "No, the store came first. But my father had always dreamed of owning his own restaurant. He didn't have the money so his parents helped them out."

"The ones who built the beach house?"

Jordan nodded. "My mother's parents were older when they had her. I think in their forties. So when they retired, they moved to Arizona. Growing up, we rarely saw them," she said.

"Why Arizona?"

"Both of my mother's siblings lived there. They were older and already had kids when my parents got married. So they went where the grandkids were."

"So you were never close to them?"

"No. When I think of family, it's my dad's parents. But he's an only child, so cousins and whatnot are all in Arizona still."

"They came for the funeral, surely," Annie said.

"No. And we really didn't expect them to," Jordan said. "They'd seen Matt maybe three or four times in their lifetime. And my grandparents, they're both deceased."

"So you have all this family in Arizona, yet you really only have your mom and dad," she said.

"Yeah. But that's how it's always been." Jordan glanced at her. "What about you? I know you're an only child, but what about aunts and uncles?"

"I have an aunt who lives in Corpus. She divorced, never remarried and never had kids," she said. "She's my father's sister, but she doesn't come around much. Thanksgiving and Christmas, that's about it. My mother's brother lives in Houston. He's married with four kids, but they're all younger than me. He's ten years younger than my mother."

"So no close relatives for you either?"

"No. Just my parents really." She was feeling sad again. "And you know how that's going."

Jordan put one arm around her shoulder, pulled her closer for a second, then released her. "So let's have them over for dinner," she suggested again.

"It could get awkward," she warned.

"Don't you think if they knew who the father was, they might feel a little better?"

Annie stopped walking. "I'm not sure. Matt's gone. It might make it worse."

"Well, at least they won't be holding out hope that you'll marry the father of your baby."

Annie slapped her arm. "I can't believe you said that."

"I'm not making light of Matt's death," Jordan said. "But it might make them feel better if they know who the father is rather than thinking it's some thug you hooked up with in a drunken stupor on a Friday night."

Annie laughed. "Yeah, now that's *so* me."

"Come on," Jordan coaxed. "Have them out to the house. They need to get over it. *You* need to get over it."

"Me?"

"Yeah, you. It is what it is, Annie. And as we've just discussed, they're the only family you have." Jordan smiled as she met her gaze. "Well, other than me."

Annie's chest tightened at her words, and without thinking, she moved closer, wrapping her arms around Jordan's shoulders and hugging her tightly.

"Thank you," she whispered into her ear.

CHAPTER TWENTY-TWO

Annie closed the door, then leaned against it. She blew out a breath as she looked across the room to where Jordan was watching her.

"I guess it could have been worse," she said.

Jordan gave her a half-smile. "It wasn't so bad."

Annie pushed off the door. "My mother barely spoke to you."

Jordan shrugged. "Oh, well. She's probably never been in the same room with a lesbian before. Not knowingly, at least."

Annie laughed. "I'm certain of that." Her smile faded. "But still, she was rude to you in your own home."

Jordan walked closer. "Annie, it's not me they were here to see. I couldn't care less what your mother thinks of me."

Annie sighed. Yes, her mother had been blatantly rude. Surprisingly, her father had been rather cordial to Jordan. Annie met Jordan's gaze, smiling slightly. "I thought my mother was going to faint when I told her about Matt."

Jordan nodded. "I did too. But at least they know now. They can stop speculating."

"God, can you believe how many times she mentioned Derrick's name?"

Jordan poured herself a glass of wine, then looked at Annie with raised eyebrows. Annie nodded at her unasked question. After Jordan poured an apple cider for her, they took their glasses out to the deck, as had become the norm for them.

It was a warm evening and Jordan put the ceiling fan on as well as the oscillating fan she kept in the corner. Annie's shorts were tight and she unbuttoned them, letting out a relieved sigh.

"When are you going shopping?"

"I've got to go to Corpus for my doctor's appointment on Tuesday. I'll go by the mall then." She turned her head, looking at Jordan. "I can't believe I'm about to buy maternity clothes. Having kids was never really in my plans," she admitted. "Even when I was married, I had no desire to have kids. I thought it was just because of Derrick and...you know, I wanted out of the marriage."

"I know this wasn't in your plans. I know you want to finish college and get on with your life," Jordan said. "But I'm really glad you didn't get an abortion. And I'm not just saying that because it's Matt's baby."

Annie reached over and took her hand, squeezing tightly. "I never considered an abortion. I do vote pro-choice, though. I think it should be each woman's own decision."

"I agree," Jordan said. "And if you'd decided to do it, I wouldn't have judged you. But I'm glad you didn't."

Annie smiled and released her hand. No, she hadn't ever considered an abortion, despite her mother's mention of it. Talk about hypocrisy. Her mother was always first in line when her church organized pro-life rallies. She wondered if her father knew that her mother had suggested it.

"So, do you think they're pleased with your living arrangements?" Jordan asked. "I mean, your father seemed to like it here."

Annie laughed. "Pleased? My mother is afraid I'm going to catch some disease from you," she teased. "When you took Dad down to see the new pier, she hinted that if I wanted to move back in with them, I could."

"Really? And?"

"I told her it was far too relaxing and stress-free here for me to even consider moving back with them."

"Good. Because I like you being here," Jordan said. "I've always lived alone. I wasn't really sure what to expect."

"I didn't either," Annie admitted. "I mean, we didn't really know each other all that well when I moved in." She again reached over and took Jordan's hand. She no longer tried to analyze why she had this compelling need to touch her as much as she did. "You've become a good friend, Jordan. I could only imagine the mental state I'd be in if it weren't for you."

Jordan surprised her by linking their fingers together. "Thank you. Having you here has made me realize how very few friends I really have," she said. "Work friends, mostly. Superficial. I guess I never took the time to nurture friendships. I was more interested in my career."

"You must have made friends in college."

"Sure. And there's a few that I keep up with. But it's only the occasional email or a rare phone call, that's about it. They've drifted away, like I have."

Annie felt sorry for her. What a lonely existence it must have been for her to spend so much time working and so little time playing. She'd venture to guess that this summer—despite Matt's death—had been one of the most sociable ones for Jordan in years. Not only was she interacting with them at the store, she was interacting with customers and with other shop owners. Jordan had seemed to really enjoy herself at the festival the other week, and next Sunday she was hosting the office party out here. The weeks had been full and busy and they were flying by. August would be here in no time. And August meant changes were ahead. Annie would go back to school late in the month and Jordan…well, Jordan would disappear out of her life and go back to Chicago. That thought made her very sad.

She glanced over at Jordan, realizing that they were still holding hands. She should pull away, but she didn't. It felt nice to…to connect with Jordan like this. She let her thumb rub lightly against Jordan's soft skin and Jordan tightened her fingers a bit.

Sadness gripped her again. What would she do when Jordan left? She didn't worry about a place to live. Both Jordan and her parents had made it clear that she could continue to live out here. But Jordan had become her rock. Jordan was strong, she was steady and mature. She was confident and sure of herself and Annie felt secure just being in her presence.

"What are you thinking about?" Jordan asked, her voice soft and quiet in the darkness.

"You," Annie said honestly.

Jordan said nothing. But now it was her thumb moving against Annie's skin as their hands remained linked. Annie closed her eyes, letting Jordan's gentle touch lull her into an even deeper sense of peacefulness.

CHAPTER TWENTY-THREE

When the office door burst open, Annie looked up sharply from the order she was placing. She silently groaned as Derrick stood there. She knew by the look on his face that he'd heard the news.

"What the hell, Annie?"

She closed the laptop without finishing the order, knowing Derrick would not be satisfied by a quick explanation.

"You ever heard of knocking?" she asked. "And you shouldn't even be back here in the first place."

"Quit stalling," he said. "Tell me it's not true."

"Are you referring to my pregnancy? Or who the father is?"

His jaw dropped open. "Jesus, you really *are* pregnant?"

"It's not any of your concern, Derrick. Or your business," she said bluntly.

He closed the door, then turned to her. She was surprised by the anger in his eyes. "You going to tell me how this happened?"

"Like I said, it's not any of your business."

"The hell it's not," he said loudly. "I wanted to have a kid with you, but no, that never worked out, did it? And now I find out that you were sleeping with Matt Sims. He was my *friend*. And you were fucking him."

Annie stood up. "Get out of my office." She pointed at the door. "Now."

"You're nothing but a goddamn slut, Annie." He laughed, but it was hardly jovial. "And now you're living with his gay sister. What the hell is wrong with you?"

For the first time in all the years that she'd known Derrick, she was actually afraid of him. There was a look in his eyes that she'd never seen before. She didn't know if he was in any mood to be reasoned with.

"You and I," she said, pointing between them, "are divorced. You and I are nothing to each other. Nothing," she said. "We're not friends. Nothing. You have no right to come in here and speak to me like this."

He slammed his fist down on the desk. "You're pregnant with Matt Sims's baby!"

"Yes, I am."

"It should be mine."

She held her hands up. "Why? Why should it be yours?"

"Because I still love you, Annie. I do."

She shook her head. "Oh, Derrick, you don't love me. We were high school *kids*. We had no business getting married in the first place," she said.

She was thankful some of the anger left his face. He ran his hands through his dark hair, then plunged them in his pockets.

"How long were you and Matt...sleeping together?"

She realized Derrick was more hurt than angry. Should she tell him the truth? Should she tell him it was only the one night? She didn't feel the need to lie to him.

"We weren't dating, Derrick. It was only a one-night thing," she said.

He met her gaze. "One night?"

"Yes."

"One night? One night and you get pregnant? Hell, I tried for six years to get you pregnant. Matt gets it done in one night."

"Derrick, don't read more into this than it is. I got pregnant. It's something I have to deal with. It has nothing to do with you."

He stared at her for the longest time before speaking. "Tell me, Annie, did you ever want kids with me?"

She didn't want to hurt him any more than he already was. So for that question, she did lie. "Yes. At the beginning, yes."

"Yet you never got pregnant." His tone was slightly accusing, and if he point-blank asked her if she had ever gotten off the pill, she wasn't sure if she'd tell him the truth or not.

"It was probably for the best, seeing as how our marriage didn't last," she said.

"The best for who?"

"The best for me, Derrick."

"Yeah. I guess." He shrugged. "What are you going to do now?"

"I'm going to finish school like I'd planned."

He nodded, then he looked pointedly at her belly. "You're not showing yet."

She smiled. "I'm hiding it. I haven't told everyone yet."

He again ran a hand through his hair. "Look, you and me. That kid's going to need a father. Maybe we could—"

"No."

"Hear me out, Annie. I think—"

"No, Derrick. And I know this is my mother putting these thoughts in your head," she said. "I'm okay alone. I'm going to be fine. Matt's parents are very supportive. They'll be there for me. Jordan's been great. She's—"

"A lesbian," he said. "What the hell are you doing living with a lesbian?"

"Jordan and I are friends, Derrick. She's been good for me. I owe her so much. Don't pass judgment," she said.

"You don't think people will talk? Will speculate about what kind of a relationship you have with her?"

"Oh, come on. Who? The people at my mother's church?"

"For starters," he said.

"I don't really care what they think. It's none of their business. I don't belong to that church."

"And you're going to raise this kid alone?"

"Like I said, I have support. Something my own parents haven't given me."

"Oh, hell, Annie. You mother is still in shock over the whole thing. She says she cries every day over it."

Annie rolled her eyes. "I would imagine that's a bit of an exaggeration. She's embarrassed more than anything."

"And do you like doing that to her?"

Annie laughed. "Oh, Derrick, really? Did she coach you on what to say?"

Derrick shook his head. "She said that you'd changed. I guess it's true."

"I haven't changed." She paused. "Well, maybe I have. The whole time living at home with them I was never able to…to spread my wings," she said. "I went from living with them in high school to living with you. Then I went back to living with them. It was a mistake, but I couldn't afford a place of my own."

"Your mistake was leaving me."

"No, Derrick. That was the best decision I could have made. For me and for you. I wasn't happy and I wasn't making you happy. You know that."

"We never even tried counseling."

"And there's a reason we didn't. I'm sorry, Derrick. It was never your fault. You didn't do anything wrong. It was always me," she said.

"And there's no chance for us…ever?"

"No. You need to quit thinking there is. You need to find you somebody and get on with your life."

He shrugged. "How come we never talked like this before?"

"You weren't receptive to it," she said. She walked around the desk and faced him. "Don't waste any more years, Derrick. You'll make someone a good husband."

He nodded. "I'm sorry I called you a slut."

She smiled. "It's okay. I know I'm not one. It's only the truth that hurts."

"You'll let me know if you need anything? I mean, you know, maybe the kid will need someone to teach him how to play baseball or something."

"We'll see." She reached for the door and held it open for him, stepping aside so he could pass.

"Take care of yourself, Annie. Like I said, let me know if you need anything."

"Thank you. I will."

As soon as the back door to the store closed, she let out a relieved breath. She knew she'd have to have this talk with him, and truthfully, it had gone better than she'd anticipated. She went back to the desk and opened up the laptop again. Her session with the retailer had timed out, losing her order. She logged in again, feeling a lightness in her mood, something she rarely felt after a visit with Derrick. She only hoped Derrick would relay their conversation to her mother. Maybe then she'd give up on the hope of them getting back together. Because that was never going to happen.

But thoughts of her mother dampened her good mood a bit. How long was she going to punish her over this? How long would it take before she embraced her? Would she ever?

* * *

Jordan came in the front door carrying a large bag from Pepe's. She'd run across the street for lunch and noticed that Brandon was still talking to the same young woman as when she'd left. Well, she was cute. She couldn't blame him. But there were other customers in the store, and Molly was working the cash register. So she walked over to him with a questioning look on her face.

"Hey, boss. Glad you're here. Two things. First, I want you to meet Kensi."

Jordan smiled politely. "Hello, Kensi." She turned to Brandon. "What's going on?"

He grinned. "Well, I'm working, of course."

"Uh-huh."

"Really. I met Kensi at the festival." He pointed to a handful of prints she held. "Local artist. What do you think about carrying some of her stuff?"

"Yeah?"

"I mean, I didn't promise her anything. I'm just looking at them. But she's really talented."

Jordan looked over at Kensi, who had been standing by silently. "Let me take a look." She put the food bag down and took a couple of prints from her. They were the originals, all done in watercolors. Different birds, of which Jordan could only identify the heron and the whooping crane. They appeared to be very good to her untrained eye.

"These are good," she said. "I'm assuming you'll make copies of these and sell them as numbered prints? Maybe signed copies?"

"Yeah. Like limited editions," Brandon said. "What do you think, boss?"

"What all do you have? Just watercolors?" she asked Kensi.

"I have some in pencil too. Oil and acrylic. Watercolor is my favorite medium though."

Jordan nodded. "Okay, sure. Why not. We'll give it a try."

"Great!" Brandon turned to Kensi. "See? I told you she was super cool."

Super cool? God, had she ever been called "super cool" before? Jordan smiled as she picked up her lunch bag. "What else?" she asked, still smiling. "You said you had two things."

"Oh, yeah. Derrick Dockery was here." He motioned to the back. "In the office. Molly said he was yelling."

"Yelling?" Jordan narrowed her eyes. "At Annie?"

"Yeah. I told her to listen at the door, but she was scared to."

Jordan felt her jaw clench. "Is he still here?"

"No, he left. But Annie hasn't come out."

"Okay. Thanks."

Jordan hurried to the back. She'd promised Annie that she would be here when Derrick confronted her. She only hoped he hadn't been too much of an ass. The office door was closed, and she knocked twice before opening it. Annie was not sitting behind the desk. Instead, she was on the sofa, looking a little somber.

"You okay? I heard you had a visitor," she said.

Annie sighed. "Yeah."

"Molly heard yelling."

"Oh, just a little."

Jordan set their lunch on the desk, then she sat down beside Annie on the sofa. "Want to talk?"

Annie sighed again. "It's not really Derrick that's got me blue," she said. "Although he did call me a slut."

"I'm sorry," she said. She draped an arm around Annie's shoulder, and Annie leaned against her.

"That hurt. I pretended it didn't, but it did."

"Need me to go beat him up for you?"

Annie smiled. "That would be a sight." Annie turned her head to look at her. "It's all good with him though. I think he finally realizes that we're not ever getting back together."

"Then what's wrong?"

"My mother. She's the one who told him. And some of the things he said, well, they obviously came from her mouth." She leaned closer to Jordan. "It's just so depressing, Jordan. I know she's embarrassed about me being pregnant, but it's not like I'm sixteen or anything."

"I know."

"And she's not in the least bit excited about being a grandmother. How can she shun me like this? I keep thinking that she's going to come around, you know?"

"She will."

"I don't think so. I didn't tell you this, but last week when I had my doctor's appointment, I asked her to go along. I told her I needed to go shopping for maternity clothes and I wanted her help." Annie shook her head. "She said she was too busy."

"Oh, honey, I'm sorry," Jordan said. "I would have gone with you."

"I know you would have. I made Suzanne go with me. We had fun. But still...my mother was too busy for me." Annie buried her face against Jordan. "It's breaking my heart."

Jordan wrapped both arms around her and held her tight. She heard sniffling and knew Annie was crying. That sound tugged at her heart, and she pulled Annie even closer, feeling a profound need to protect her.

"The only thing you can do, Annie, is keep trying. We can have them out to dinner again."

"Oh, yeah, the last time was so much fun," she mumbled.

Jordan smiled and kissed Annie's head. "Maybe we should have my parents over at the same time. They know each other."

Annie pulled away. "Your parents are *normal*," she said. "I would be embarrassed for them to see my parents like this. Because honestly, I never thought they would have this reaction." She wiped a tear from her cheek. "I knew they would be upset, but I thought it would pass. I thought eventually they would be excited. I mean, I'm almost thirty. It's not like I have a whole lot of years left to have kids." Annie slammed her hand against Jordan's thigh. "And all those years with Derrick, she practically *begged* me to give her a grandchild. Now she acts like *this*?"

Okay, so Annie was getting pissed. Well, Jordan thought, that was better than feeling guilty and hurt.

"Maybe you should tell her that," Jordan suggested.

Annie sighed. "I'm sorry. God, my hormones are all over the place," she said with a wave of her hand. "I'm not normally a crier." She smiled at Jordan. "You're so good to me. Why is that?"

Jordan shrugged. "We're friends."

Jordan felt her breath catch as Annie leaned closer, brushing her lips against Jordan's cheek. Jordan didn't breathe again until Annie pulled away.

"Thank you for being here."

"You're welcome."

Their eyes held for a long moment, then Annie smiled. "Did you get extra cheese on my enchiladas?"

"I got extra *everything* for you," Jordan said.

CHAPTER TWENTY-FOUR

Annie stood at the corner of the deck, watching Jordan and Brandon untie the Jet Ski. Jordan was in her typical bikini top and water shorts. Annie was used to seeing her like that now, but she found herself staring at her nonetheless. God, it was like she had a crush on her or something.

Of course, she already suspected that. Who knew her crazy hormones would lead her in this direction? As if sensing her watching, Jordan looked up. Annie matched her smile, feeling her pulse race just a little. At that, she wondered what the hell was wrong with her. But despite that thought, she didn't take her eyes off Jordan as she stood in the water next to the pier.

"Hey, girl."

Annie blinked several times, finally turning her attention to Suzanne. "Hey. Glad you came," she said, moving closer for a quick hug.

Suzanne's gaze followed Annie's back to the bay. "What are you staring at? Brandon's a little young for you, isn't he?"

Annie hoped she wasn't blushing. "Nothing. Just...lost in thought."

Suzanne leaned on the railing much like Annie was doing. "So how's it going with Jordan? You still like living here?"

"It's good. She's been great."

"No quirks?"

Annie smiled. "You mean because she's gay? No. I like her a lot. She's been so good to me."

"Because of Matt?"

"What do you mean?"

"I mean, because she's his sister."

Annie shook her head. "No, I don't think that really has anything to do with it. We just clicked, right off the bat. You know, you meet someone out of the blue and you hit it off. It's been like that with us," she said. "We fell into a friendship and it's been...well, easy." Annie paused, afraid she was saying too much. "Jordan's been here for me through all this," she said. "And she hasn't blinked. Nothing seems to throw her off."

"I should have been here for you more," Suzanne said.

Annie waved her apology away. "No, that's not what I was implying. You and Aaron are friends with Derrick. I wouldn't want to put you in the middle of that," she said. "Derrick flipped out, like you said he would. And my mother is still out of the picture. She barely speaks to me." She shrugged. "And every day, Jordan is there. She's...steady. She makes me feel like everything is going to be okay. No matter what, she's always... steady." Annie looked back to the bay, watching as Jordan and Brandon made their way back up to the house.

"So where's Britney?" she asked, changing the subject.

"Oh, Jessica took her. They're inside watching TV." Suzanne smiled at her. "Well, you look good, Annie. You look happy."

Annie smiled too. "Thanks. I feel good. And I am happy."

"You're not wearing one of the new blouses we picked out," Suzanne noted.

Annie looked at the oversized tank she had on over her bikini top. "I know. I'm going to tell everyone today. I can't hide it much longer," she said, touching her belly.

"Are you getting more excited?"

"Actually, I kinda am," she admitted. "I might as well. It's not like it's going away," she said with a laugh.

Jordan and Brandon came up on the deck, and Brandon pointed at her. "Are you ready to take a spin?"

Annie shook her head. "No way. Not after last year. You almost drowned me."

Brandon laughed. "I rescued you right away."

"Take Molly," she suggested. Molly had been sitting at the other end of the deck reading a book. She looked up when she heard her name mentioned.

"You want to?" Brandon offered.

"I've never been on one before," Molly said.

"I promise I'll go slow," Brandon said.

Annie laughed. "Don't trust him," she said. She turned to Jordan. "Suzanne brought Britney, her daughter. Maybe you could take her out later."

"Of course," Jordan said. "I'm going to check on Staci and see how the margarita machine is coming along. Suzanne, would you like one?"

"Sure. But I'll come inside. I probably need to rescue Jessica."

"Apple cider?" Jordan asked her.

"Just a bottle of water, thanks."

Jordan nodded and touched Annie's arm briefly as she passed by. Such a simple touch, yet Annie felt it all the way down to her toes.

She turned her gaze back to the bay, barely registering Brandon and Molly as they sped away from shore. Her thoughts were solely on Jordan—Jordan and these crazy feelings she was having. Crazy, yes. She was pregnant with Matt's baby and she had a crush on his lesbian sister.

Just having a crush on someone—anyone—was unusual for her. But Jordan? A *woman*?

Crazy.

* * *

Jordan hadn't been too keen on the margarita machine, considering Molly and Steven were still in high school and Jessica hadn't even reached her twentieth birthday yet. But

Annie had talked her into it. Two of Brandon's buddies were coming later, and Staci had brought her boyfriend. Still, she would limit it to only one batch. Maybe she was being paranoid, but she didn't want anyone to overdo it.

"God, I'm getting old," she murmured.

"Still worried about them drinking too much?"

Jordan turned, finding Annie watching her. She smiled at her. "Yeah. I need to relax, I know."

"They're all responsible. They'll be fine. Besides, Staci is going to make up a pitcher of nonalcoholic margaritas for those under twenty-one."

Jordan nodded. "Good. So did Brandon really leave a box of Fat Larry T-shirts out by the door?"

"He said since we were closing the store early, he wanted to leave something as a prize. He put out the ones with the old design on them," Annie said. "He did ask me first. I hope it's okay."

"You're the manager," Jordan reminded her.

Annie bumped her shoulder with her own. "Yeah, but you're the boss."

Jordan touched the hem of Annie's tank top and tugged on it. "You look nice," she said. That was an understatement. Annie looked beautiful.

Annie's eyes held hers. "Thank you." Annie took her hand and squeezed it. "You look nice too," she said quietly, her gaze drifting downward.

Jordan's breath caught and she dared not speak. Annie smiled and dropped her hand, then left without another word. What the hell was going on with them? The touching? The looks between them? Now *flirting*?

Jordan's hand was trembling. She set her beer bottle down, escaping out to the deck. Molly was reading, sitting off by herself. Jordan didn't interrupt her. She headed down the deck steps, needing some time alone. Brandon had taken Jessica out on the Jet Ski so she walked to the end of the pier and plopped down on the wooden bench.

So, okay, she liked Annie. As a *friend*. Nothing more. Well, maybe there was a tiny bit of attraction there, but nothing she couldn't handle. But what she *couldn't* handle was Annie flirting with her. Did Annie even know what she was doing? Of course not. Annie was just being Annie. She was affectionate. She liked to touch. She liked to hug. She liked to kiss Jordan on the cheek.

Jordan leaned back against the pier, staring out across the water. Yeah, and she liked all of those things now too.

"She's pregnant with Matt's baby," she reminded herself. She couldn't possibly be attracted to her. That would just be…crazy.

CHAPTER TWENTY-FIVE

Annie was nervous as she looked around at everyone. But she couldn't put it off any longer. Was it something to say over dinner though? She looked over at Jordan and found her watching. Jordan gave her a reassuring nod, chasing some of her nervousness away. She put down her half-eaten fajita and stood up.

"I have some news," she said. Everyone stopped eating and looked at her. She decided the best thing to do was blurt it out. So she did just that. "I'm…I'm going to have a baby."

It was a shocked silence that greeted her statement.

"You mean…like adopt?" Staci asked.

Annie touched her belly. "No…like I'm pregnant."

"Oh, wow."

"Yeah, wow," Jessica said. "I didn't even know you were dating anyone."

Annie looked over at Jordan, who sported an amused expression. "I'm not dating anyone," she said.

"Oh, my God," Staci said. "Sperm bank?"

At that, Jordan laughed, and Annie nearly rolled her eyes. "No."

"Well, then, what's going on?" Jessica asked.

Annie blew out her breath. "Look, let's just get it all out in the open, okay." She again looked at Jordan. "Matt. Matt is the father."

Again, silence. And again, Staci was the one to break it.

"You mean *our* Matt?"

Annie nodded. "Yes. Our Matt."

Staci's eyes widened. "You were dating *Matt*?"

"No. We were *not* dating."

"Oh, cool, Annie," Jessica said. "You were fuck buddies? I would have never guessed that was your style."

Annie stared at her, shocked. She felt a blush on her face and knew she'd turned beet red. "No…we were not…*buddies* of any sort." God, whose idea was it to tell them? She shook her head. "Look, the whys and hows of it don't matter," she said. "I wanted you to know because I can't hide it much longer."

She lifted up the end of her tank, showing off the baby bump that her maternity shorts could not conceal.

"Well, I thought you'd gained weight," Staci said bluntly.

Annie turned slowly, looking at Jordan with raised eyebrows as she let her tank top cover her again. Jordan smiled at her and said what she always said.

"You're not fat."

"Uh-huh." Annie motioned to the table. "So enjoy the rest of your meal and please don't gossip about me."

"Nothing to gossip about," Brandon said. "Congratulations."

"Thank you."

She sat down again and Suzanne nudged her. "That wasn't so bad."

"Am I getting fat?" she whispered.

"No. She was being petty. You know she always had a crush on Matt."

"I know." She picked up her fajita again. Even Staci's comment didn't curb her appetite.

* * *

Annie put the last of the leftovers in the fridge and wiped down the counter. Suzanne had stayed late and helped them clean up but she, too, had taken her leave. It was quiet in the house, and she found Jordan sitting out on the deck in the dark, sipping from her wineglass. She was about to flip on the porch light, then decided not to.

"So you survived?" she asked as she sat down beside her.

"Glad it's over with," Jordan said. "They seemed to have fun though."

"Yes, they did."

"Did you?"

"It was okay. But things like this remind you that even though you work together, it doesn't always mean that you're friends," she said.

"True."

Annie leaned closer. "You're being awful quiet. Is everything okay?"

Jordan turned toward her, but it was too dark to read her eyes.

"Fine. I just wanted some peace."

"Oh. I'm sorry. I shouldn't have—"

Jordan reached out and wrapped her fingers around Annie's arm. "Not from you, Annie."

"Are you sure?"

"Yes. Stay."

Annie felt Jordan's fingers slip away from her, and she had to resist reaching out and taking her hand. Instead, she folded her hands together and rested them on her stomach. She let the quiet wash over her, listening to the sound of the water as it lapped against the retaining wall. The breeze rustled her hair, but before she could tame it, Jordan gently moved it from her face and tucked it behind her ear.

Annie turned, again wishing she could see Jordan's eyes. She swallowed, imagining what she might find there. She looked back over the dark bay, enjoying the closeness she felt with Jordan, even in their silence.

They sat there for the longest time, the only sound to break the quiet the occasional bark of a dog and the constant waves hitting the pier. She was relaxed and mellow and felt her eyelids getting heavy.

"I think I'm going to bed," she said finally.

Jordan turned. "I'll be in soon."

Annie stood, then leaned over, kissing Jordan lightly on the cheek. "Thank you. It was a nice day."

Jordan smiled. "It was a nicer evening."

Annie smiled too, squeezing Jordan's shoulder as she left.

CHAPTER TWENTY-SIX

It was a rare rainy evening and instead of their normal routine of sitting on the deck after dinner, they were inside. Annie was on the sofa, legs curled under her, reading a book. Jordan was in the recliner, aimlessly flipping through TV channels, not finding anything to hold her attention. When her phone rang, she was thankful for the distraction. However, she was surprised by the caller.

"It's Peter," she said.

Annie raised her eyebrows.

"My boss," she clarified before answering. "Hello, Peter."

"Ah, Jordan. I was afraid you weren't going to answer. You've been a bit of a stranger this summer."

She went out to the deck, standing under the porch to keep from getting wet from the light rain that was still falling. "I assumed Antonio was handling things," she said. "He hasn't called for help."

"Yes, he's handling things. He just doesn't do them your way," he said. "I expected you back by now."

"I told you it would probably be September. Is there a problem?"

"Tokyo."

"Tokyo? I thought that deal was wrapped up," she said.

"All but the fine print. But Mr. Hashimoto refuses to deal with Antonio."

Jordan smiled. Mr. Hashimoto was brutal in negotiations, but she'd managed to soften him up. It had taken six months, but he'd finally agreed to her terms. She could imagine him and Antonio butting heads.

"And you want me to run interference?"

"I need you back here, Jordan. We can't let this deal fall through. He's threatening to pull out."

"I can't come back now, Peter," she said. She looked through the window, finding Annie watching her. "Perhaps I can handle it from here."

"No," he said. "I need you here in the office. Can you at least come back for a few days? Help Antonio through this? Mr. Hashimoto respects you. You were on the team that put this deal together."

She let out a heavy sigh. "When?"

"Now."

She knew she didn't really have a choice. "Okay."

"Thanks, Jordan. I knew I could count on you. I was so sure of it, I've already booked your flight. Check your email."

"Does that mean I'm leaving tomorrow?"

"Yes. Don't sleep in."

She slipped the phone into her shorts pocket. She didn't want to leave, not even for a few days. What the hell was she going to do when September got here?

The rain had turned into nothing more than a fine mist, and she walked out in it, leaning on the railing. No, she didn't want to leave. She would miss it here. She would miss…Annie. Hell, she would even miss Fat Larry.

She looked out over the bay, the light on the pier surrounded by fog. God, what was wrong with her? It was only for a few days. Then she'd come back, she'd tie things up, she'd hire someone to take over the store…then she'd be gone for good. She closed her eyes to that thought. Not for good. Not this time. She wouldn't disappear this time. She wouldn't do that to her parents again.

She turned when she heard the door open. Annie was watching her. She moved closer, close enough for their shoulders to touch as they leaned on the railing together.

"You're leaving?" The question was asked quietly, almost as if she didn't want to hear the answer.

"Yes."

Annie turned to face her. "Will you come back?" This time, the question was little more than a whisper.

Jordan turned too, leaving them face-to-face. She nodded. "Yes. I'm only going for a couple of days."

The relief in Annie's eyes was palpable. "I'm not…ready for you to leave yet, Jordan."

Jordan nodded. "No, I'm not ready to leave either."

"Is there a problem or something?"

"Yeah, a client in Tokyo. He doesn't want to work with my assistant. It's just wrapping up a deal that I worked on in the spring," she said.

"Oh."

"It should only take a couple of days," she said again.

Annie nodded, but Jordan still saw doubt in her eyes. Without thinking, she pulled Annie closer. Annie didn't hesitate and her arms snaked around Jordan's waist. As soon as Annie was pressed against her, Jordan knew it was a mistake. They had hugged before, of course. But never quite with the intimacy of this hug. She wondered if Annie could feel the energy between them.

"We really need to stop doing this," she said, her eyes still closed as Annie's face was buried against her neck.

"Why?" Annie murmured.

"I think you know why."

Annie pulled back but only enough to meet her eyes. "Do I?"

"We're awfully close to that line, Annie."

Annie's smile was slow, sweet. "I think we've already crossed the line, Jordan."

Jordan smiled too. "Mentally, yes."

Annie pulled away a little more but didn't completely untangle from her. Her eyes were open and honest, and Jordan tried to decipher what she saw there.

"Something's...happening to me," Annie said. "I feel... different."

"Does that frighten you?"

"No...yes...maybe a little," she said with a smile.

Jordan reached out, brushing her fingers across Annie's cheek, then lower, caressing her lips with the barest of touches.

"You know you never, ever have to be afraid of me," she said.

Annie swallowed. "It's hardly you I'm afraid of, Jordan." She smiled slightly. "Maybe you should be afraid of me."

Jordan smiled too. "Oh, that, I definitely am."

Annie took another step away from her, breaking their contact.

"So? You're leaving. When?"

Jordan sighed. "Tomorrow. He already had my flight booked."

"And you'll be back home when?"

Home? Yes, this did feel like home. When had that happened?

"Hopefully on Saturday," she said.

"Well, you don't have to worry about the store. I'll take care of it."

"I'm not worried," she said.

Annie nodded, then motioned to the house. "I think I'm going to shower and get to bed early."

Jordan nodded. "Sure."

Annie made it to the door, then stopped. Jordan held her breath as Annie walked back over to her. She leaned closer, kissing Jordan...not on the cheek, like she usually did. Not on the lips, either. No, on the corner of her mouth, just enough to let Jordan know that they had indeed crossed over the line.

"Goodnight, Jordan."

"Goodnight."

Jordan stood still, watching as Annie went back inside. She turned around to the bay again. What was happening? Her pulse was racing, her heart was pounding and she had a difficult time catching her breath. Oh, she knew exactly what was happening.

Did Annie?

CHAPTER TWENTY-SEVEN

Annie stared at the laptop, her chin resting in the palm of her hand. She couldn't seem to concentrate on the inventory this week. Oh, who was she kidding? Had she even *tried* to do inventory? No. All she could see was Jordan driving away that morning.

In the light of day, they'd both been a little…well, she didn't want to say distant, but perhaps more careful with what they said, what they did. She still couldn't believe she'd kissed Jordan like she had. What in the world had she been thinking?

She leaned back in the office chair and stared at the ceiling. She knew exactly what she'd been thinking. She nearly panicked at the thought of Jordan leaving. The intimacy of the hug they shared had been so…so sweet, so innocent and yet so very thrilling it made her pulse race. She couldn't remember a time—ever—in her life where a hug from someone had made her feel like that. Something about Jordan caused her to…to crave her touch, made her want to touch Jordan, to be close to her. And the kiss? She'd be lying to herself if she said it had been an accident that she'd brushed Jordan's lips with her own. Shocked by her actions? Sure. Jordan had been as well.

And this morning they'd not mentioned it. Jordan had been packing, and she'd made a quick breakfast for her even though Jordan had told her not to bother. Bacon and toast were hardly a bother. They'd shared breakfast and coffee and made small talk, nothing more. Jordan promised to call her and Annie had promised to take care of the inventory and ordering for the week. She'd walked out with Jordan and right before Jordan had gotten in her SUV, she'd pulled Annie into a tight, quick hug. They'd stared at each other, but no words were exchanged. Annie had been shocked that she'd felt tears threaten when watching Jordan drive away.

"Damn hormones," she murmured.

Yes, indeed. Damn hormones. They apparently were wreaking havoc on a number of her senses.

She shook off her thoughts, trying to turn her focus to the inventory instead. It had to get done. Not only had she promised Jordan she'd handle both it and the ordering, Brandon had told her they were nearly out of the "I'd Rather Be at the Beach" T-shirts that were so popular, as well as popcorn supplies. She ordered the popcorn supplies first. As Matt had told her many times, *never* run out of popcorn.

She managed to put Jordan from her mind as she went about her office tasks, again thankful for the interface Steven had done with the inventory. It made it so much easier to place orders. She'd just pulled up the last vendor's website when the back door to the store opened. She expected Brandon and was surprised to see Loraine, Jordan's mother, smiling at her.

"Annie, hi. I hope I'm not interrupting."

"I was about to place our last order for the week." It was then she saw the familiar Subway bags.

Loraine held them up. "I understand Jordan had to go to Chicago unexpectedly. I brought lunch, if you're interested," she said.

Annie smiled at her. She'd only seen Loraine once since they'd had them out for dinner, and that was one Saturday when she and Jordan had gone to the restaurant for lunch. She assumed Loraine's presence here now was Jordan's doing.

"That was thoughtful of you," Annie said. "Please come in."

"The office looks completely different," Loraine said as she looked around. "No clutter, for one thing." She glanced at the sofa. "This is new, right?"

"Yes. Jordan replaced the old one. It was…well, rather worn," she said, hoping she wasn't blushing. Since Jordan had brought in the new leather sofa, Annie no longer had visions of that night with Matt. However, Loraine's mention of the old sofa brought them back in an instant.

Loraine nodded. "Well, finish with your order. I need to wash up."

"It'll only take me a second," she said. "There are water bottles in the fridge out there."

"I'll grab a couple."

Annie made quick work of her order, clicking the submit button just as Loraine came back in. She closed the laptop, then joined Loraine on the sofa.

"I hadn't even thought about lunch," Annie admitted. "Jordan usually takes care of that for me."

Loraine laughed. "Which is probably why she suggested I come by."

Annie smiled. "I figured she had something to do with it."

"She was rather evasive on the phone. Do you know why she had to go back?"

"Some client in Tokyo," Annie said. "Apparently things weren't working out with her assistant."

"She's never been very forthcoming about her job," Loraine said. "I really have no idea what she even does."

Annie nodded. "No, she doesn't talk about it much at all. Based on how many hours she says she works, I imagine it's very stressful." She opened her sandwich, finding the usual turkey. It even had the added sweet banana peppers that she liked. Apparently Jordan had been exact in telling her mother what to get.

"I hope I got it right."

"Perfect. I don't know why, but I've been craving peppers lately."

"I had the weirdest cravings when I was pregnant. Onions, of all things. I could practically eat them like an apple," she said with a laugh. "And when I was pregnant with Matt, I went through a whole month where I ate pineapple slices on my hamburger, which I had nearly daily. Then one day I had it and it was the nastiest thing I'd ever tasted. To this day, I can't stand pineapple."

"I've had cravings for Mexican food," Annie said, "but that doesn't always sit too well with me."

"How's your morning sickness?"

"All but gone, thankfully. My doctor said after the first trimester, it should lessen."

"Do you like your doctor? Jordan tells me she's in Corpus."

"Yes, I like her. I've only been to her twice so far."

Loraine put her sandwich down in her lap. "I don't mean to pry, but has your mother become more involved?"

Annie shook her head. "Not yet. We had my parents out to the house for dinner," she said. "I thought maybe...well, they didn't know where I was living, who I was living with. I thought having them out, having them see me, might bring them around." She shook her head. "My mother can't seem to get past the fact that I'm pregnant and unmarried."

"They know Matt is the father?"

"Yes."

"And now that he's gone, that probably makes it worse for them. There's no chance of a marriage now."

Annie took a bite of her sandwich, debating whether she should tell Loraine the truth about her and Matt. She decided she didn't want her to think that they had been on the brink of marriage.

"Matt and I...well, I liked him fine. We had known each other forever, of course. But we were just together the one night," she said. "We weren't actually dating. I'm sorry if that shocks you. Or disappoints you."

"Matt was always very open about who he was dating. Quite unlike Jordan," Loraine said. "Now that I think about it, he only mentioned you in the context of the store. He always spoke so highly of you. Whatever happened between you two for that one night, it's none of my business. You were both adults."

"Thank you. I wish my mother would be as understanding."

"When the time comes, I can't imagine that she won't be excited to hold her baby grandchild in her arms. I know I can't wait," she said as she patted Annie's hand.

Annie felt near tears, and she wondered what it was about the Sims women that did that to her. "Thank you," she said again. "It means so much to me that you're as supportive as you've been. If not for you and Jordan, I don't know what I would have done."

"Jordan has always been the responsible one," Loraine said. "I guess you know that by now. She and Matt were so different growing up. She was always mature for her age and we trusted her to make her own decisions. Matt...well, he was carefree and loved to have fun. We were terrified of having him run the store at first. Jordan would have made a much better manager. The financial numbers the last couple of months prove that," she said.

"Yes, she runs a much tighter ship than Matt did," Annie said.

Loraine sighed. "I'm not sure where we went wrong with her."

Annie frowned. Was she insinuating that they'd failed in some way because Jordan was gay?

"What do you mean?"

"We were a close family. Always were. For some reason, she never felt comfortable telling us she was gay. I don't know if she inferred from our actions that we wouldn't accept her or not... but she withdrew from us and we had no idea why."

"You never guessed she was gay?"

"No, never. And when we found out—quite by accident—it was almost too late to salvage our relationship." Loraine smiled. "Thankfully, that wasn't the case. She's still so very private about her life though. I don't know if she has someone in Chicago or not. I would like to think that she's found someone to love, someone to love her." Loraine shrugged. "My subtle questions to her are always left unanswered. Like I said, she's very private."

Annie decided it wasn't her place to tell Loraine the little that she did know. She did, however, think Loraine should know why Jordan withdrew from them.

"She thought you would hate her."

"Hate her?"

"That's why she withdrew from you. That's why she went away to college. And when you found out she was gay, she said you cried. That convinced her that you did hate her. That's why she stayed away, that's why she's in Chicago."

Loraine leaned her head back. "Oh, my goodness. Yes, I cried. We surprised her at her apartment. There was…there was another girl there with her." Loraine waved her hand. "Well, I won't go into details, but you can imagine," she said. "Anyway, yes, I handled it poorly and yes, I did cry. I don't think I was crying because she was gay. I think I was crying because she seemed so lost to us."

"I'm guessing you never talked about it."

"No. Jordan wasn't much for talking. We talked *around* it," she said. "I tried to include her in everything. I invited her home for each and every holiday. It was rare that she came. And when I suggested that we visit her up there, she was never receptive to it."

"She and Matt were close growing up?"

"Yes. Matt adored her. It didn't faze him in the least that she was gay." Loraine folded up the rest of her sandwich. "After his accident, we weren't sure what to expect from Jordan. When she offered to come stay here, offered to take care of things, it was such a relief. And having her here this summer has made us realize how much we've missed her." Loraine turned to her. "We love having her here. It's going to be so hard once she leaves again, but I know she's got her life now in Chicago."

Annie nodded. Yes, it was going to be very hard. So hard, she didn't dare even think about it.

"You know, you're starting to show more. That maternity blouse looks pretty on you."

Annie smiled, wondering if the change in subject was intentional or not. "Thank you. I finally went shopping for new clothes. These shorts are so much more comfortable than my old ones," she said. "I was having to unbutton them, they were getting so tight."

"You should have let me take you," Loraine said. "You shouldn't have to bear the financial brunt of this, Annie."

"I'm okay. This is my problem, not yours. You're not responsible for this."

"Nonsense. As Jordan said, it took two. My son is responsible for this. And if Matt were still here, it would be his problem and he'd be expected to help you." She patted Annie's hand. "I shouldn't say problem. It's a blessing, really. And we want to help," she said. "Your expenses will add up before you know it."

"I'm living with Jordan and not paying rent," she said. "I'm working full time this summer. I've been able to save. So I'm doing okay."

"Well, even if you are okay, you still won't have to face the financial burden all by yourself. We're going to help."

Loraine reached in her purse and pulled out some folded bills. Annie saw the top bill was a hundred and she shook her head.

"Loraine, I can't accept that."

"Annie, it's not much. A few hundred dollars. Just something to help with your new clothes or whatever." She smiled. "Please take it. That's my grandchild you're carrying."

Annie gave in, taking the money from her. Loraine squeezed her hand. "We want to help you in any way we can. Jordan has already told us that once you go back to part-time, we're still going to carry you on the insurance at the store."

"Really? Jordan never said anything to me."

"Yes. She told us that weeks ago. And it's as it should be. We need to help in whatever way we can. Please don't hesitate to ask us for anything, because honestly, Annie, I'm so, so happy about this baby. I think it's a wonderful thing." She smiled. "You probably didn't think so at first and I know you're most likely scared…being alone and having a baby. But just know that we'll be there for you and we will help you with anything you need. You can count on us."

Annie felt tears in her eyes and she tried to swallow them down. "Thank you. I don't know what to say…but thank you."

A tear ran down her cheek and she wiped it away. *Damn hormones.*

CHAPTER TWENTY-EIGHT

Jordan stood at the window, staring out at the high-rise office building across from hers. It was a view she'd admired for years. Well, maybe not admired. She'd rarely taken the time. Her corner office, though, was coveted by the others on her staff. She half expected Antonio to have staked a claim to it in her absence. Actually, it looked undisturbed, and she wondered if anyone had even set foot in there since she'd been gone.

Gone. Yes, she'd been gone, both physically and mentally. She'd actually been surprised at how easily she'd been able to forget about her job. It was rare when it even crossed her mind at all.

Yet here she was, falling back into the swing of things after being away for most of the summer. Three months. And she'd slipped back into her business suit, had swiped her security card at the door, had taken the elevator up to the twenty-second floor like she had never been away. And she had handled Tokyo and Mr. Hashimoto in less than two hours.

And now she wanted to go home. Back to Rockport. Back to Fat Larry's. Back to Pelican's Landing.

Back to Annie.

She closed her eyes. *Annie*. It was a dangerous game they were playing. But truth be told, she hadn't been this attracted to anyone in years. Something about Annie—her innocence, maybe—drew her and Jordan had an almost overwhelming desire to protect her. At first, she thought it was simply because Annie carried her brother's baby. But as the weeks, months, passed, she decided that wasn't the case at all. It was a physical attraction that was growing daily. It was something she had thought she could deal with. Because she had assumed it was a one-sided attraction.

The last few weeks, certainly the last few days, told her that wasn't the case at all. Annie was fighting her own battle with it. Yes, she knew Annie was confused. Who wouldn't be? She'd been married to a man for six years. She was pregnant. Now she found herself attracted to a woman. It was a situation that Jordan should run from...and fast.

Only she didn't think Annie was going to let her run. Annie wasn't quite as naïve as Jordan thought. Annie knew exactly what was going on between them.

A quick knock on her office door brought her out of her thoughts. She turned, finding Peter standing there, his expensive suit as impeccable as ever. He was a handsome man and he dressed the part. He could have just popped out of the pages of *GQ*. He was also as arrogant and vain a man as she'd ever met.

"Good job today. I knew you could handle it."

"I could have done that remotely," she said. "Why bring me all the way back here?"

"Because I wanted Antonio to learn from you. You handling it from afar would have done nothing for him." He walked farther into the office. "I really wish you would take him under your wing more, Jordan."

"I don't like him. Why would I do that?"

Peter laughed. "No, not too many do. But he's good."

"Not good enough to handle Tokyo, obviously."

"He reminds me of me," he said.

"What? Cocky?"

Peter laughed again. "You do know you're the only one who would dare speak to me like that."

She nodded. "I also know I busted my ass for this company for the last twelve years. Surely that's afforded me the right to speak my mind."

"Which you do quite often," he reminded her. "So how are things back home?"

"I've been running my brother's store. I've got to hire a manager before I come back."

"What kind of store?"

She sat down behind her desk. "It's a little souvenir-type thing. Tourist trap."

"You're kidding. That's what's been keeping you away. A souvenir shop?"

Jordan bristled. "Are you implying I'm wasting my talents?"

"Don't you think? I know what your salary is here, Jordan. Taking a leave of absence wasn't cheap."

"My parents needed me. Besides, not everything is about money, Peter. And the little souvenir shop, as you call it, does quite well."

He shook his head. "That's where you're wrong, Jordan. *Everything* is about money. Everything."

She didn't argue with him. It was something she used to believe as well. Why else had she busted her ass all these years?

"Now, I'd like you to spend some time with Antonio."

"Why?"

"Like I said, take him under your wing. Teach him."

"He's been my assistant for three years. He thinks he already knows everything," she said.

"We both know he doesn't. I thought it would take you at least two days to get Mr. Hashimoto to sign off. You've got time."

She shook her head. "No. I'm going to head back. I've got a ton of stuff to do there in the next month."

"So you're still insistent on taking the full four months? I was hoping being back here would change your mind."

"Like I said, I've got unfinished business there."

"I didn't think you were that close to your family. You rarely even mentioned them."

She shrugged. "I never mention much of anything about my private life, do I?"

"No, I don't suppose you do." He stared out her window, his face taking on a pensive look. "You know, I lost a brother once too," he said. "Many, many, many years ago." He turned, looking at her. "We were in high school. He was two years younger than me. We were on a family outing at Lake Michigan. It was a great summer day. We were playing in the water, horsing around. And one minute he was there, the next…he was gone. Drowned. Just like that." He turned his back to the window. "I always thought that my parents blamed me. They never said, but sometimes, as a kid, I could tell."

"I'm sorry," she said.

He headed toward the door, then stopped. "I sometimes forget I even had a brother. Don't let that happen to you."

"No."

He nodded. "Well, then I guess I'll let you get on with it. I'll see you in September." He raised his eyebrows. "Right?"

"Right."

He closed the door behind him, and she spun around in her chair, taking in the view out her window once more. She felt nearly stifled by it. As she'd told Annie once, she was surrounded by concrete and steel. It had become normal for her. Until now. Now, she longed for the peace and quiet of her sleepy little hometown on the Gulf Coast. Water and trees, green and blue…a salty gulf breeze, the rolling bay, pelicans and gulls.

She let out a long, slow breath, then reached for her phone. An unconscious smile lit her face as she found Annie's number. She leaned back in her chair, waiting for her to answer. She didn't have to wait long.

"Hey, you," Annie said. "I was hoping you'd call today."

The sound of Annie's voice brought a lightness to her heart and a grin to her face. "Yeah, just now got the chance. How are things?"

"Everything's fine. No issues," she said. "You?"

"Got the contract all finished. Didn't take long."

"So you're coming home?"

Home? Jordan smiled. "Yeah, I'm coming home. It'll probably be late tomorrow. I haven't made arrangements for a flight yet."

There was a slight pause. "I miss you."

Jordan's hand tightened around her cell phone. "I miss you too, Annie."

"We...we probably need to talk, huh?"

Jordan laughed quietly. "You think?"

Annie laughed too. "So...I had lunch with your mother. Thank you for that."

Jordan nodded. "You're welcome. I was afraid you'd eat nothing but popcorn."

"So now I realize how much you've spoiled me this summer," Annie said.

"Oh? You're only now realizing that?"

Annie's laugh was delightful, and Jordan couldn't get the grin off her face. They sat there in silence for a moment, listening to the other breathe. Jordan felt like an adolescent with a teenage crush.

"Listen, I need to get going," she said. "Got a few things to take care of still."

"Okay. I'm glad you called."

"I'll see you tomorrow. Like I said, it'll probably be late."

"Okay." Another pause. "Can't wait."

Jordan smiled again. "Goodbye, Annie."

"Bye, Jordan."

Jordan laid the phone on her desk and leaned back in her chair, staring at the ceiling. She was in way over her head, she knew. She hadn't realized how far Annie had gotten inside of her. It never occurred to her that their friendship would—*could*—turn into all this. It had evolved so slowly, so easily, it snuck up on her when she least expected it. Now...now she had no idea what she was going to do about it. At least Annie recognized it too. At least she wasn't blind to what was going on with them.

Maybe it would be better if she was. Maybe then, Jordan could back away. She let her eyes slip closed. No, she didn't want to back away. She wanted something that she thought she'd never have.

She sat back up and shook her head. Did she *seriously* think she could have that with Annie? Annie was carrying her brother's baby. Annie was…straight, for God's sake.

She buried her face in her hands.

"God, what am I going to do?"

No. The question was…what was Annie going to do?

CHAPTER TWENTY-NINE

Annie glanced at the clock again. It wasn't even eleven yet. Jordan had said it would be late before she got in. The day was going to be endless, she knew.

Just like the night had been. She'd made a simple dinner of black bean tacos with rice on the side. And she'd taken her solitary glass of apple cider out on the deck, but that made her miss Jordan even more, so she'd gone back inside to read. That couldn't hold her attention either, so she'd showered and was in bed before nine. Unfortunately, sleep wouldn't come and she'd tossed and turned until nearly midnight.

Tossed and turned because thoughts of Jordan were bouncing around in her head. How had this happened? How could she go from not being attracted to *anyone* to being insanely attracted to another *woman*? Was it just her hormones? Surely not. That would be so unfair.

She smiled, wondering why she wasn't frightened by her feelings. Well, as she'd told Jordan, she was a little scared. But only because it was so foreign to her. The feelings she had when she was near Jordan, when they touched…those were feelings she wanted to embrace, not run from. She wanted to embrace them because she'd never felt them before and she was afraid she'd never feel them again.

She only hoped Jordan didn't run from it.

She tapped her fingers on the desk, then closed the laptop. She had to get away and kill some time. She would drive herself crazy if she didn't. Early lunch? Maybe Suzanne had an hour free and could join her. She stopped. Maybe she should call her mother and see if she wanted to have lunch.

"God, what are you thinking?" she murmured.

No. No need to ruin the day. Not when Jordan was coming home. She called Suzanne instead.

CHAPTER THIRTY

The store was full of customers and Jordan was able to slip through it without anyone seeing her. She opened the back door and glanced toward the office. Annie was behind the desk, and she looked up when the door opened. The look of surprise—happy surprise—on Annie's face made the very early flight worthwhile.

"You're early!"

Jordan smiled. How could she not? "Yeah. Caught an early flight at dawn. Had a layover in Dallas, though."

Annie stood but didn't come any closer. Jordan closed the door and locked it. When her eyes met Annie's, she was suddenly very afraid.

"Does this mean we're going to stop pretending nothing is happening between us?"

Jordan tilted her head, watching Annie. "Have we been pretending?"

Annie walked closer to her, and Jordan felt her heart beat nervously. "I think we're past pretending, don't you?" Annie took another step toward her. "I think I would really like it if you kissed me."

Jordan felt her heart jump into her throat. She took a step back. "Here? In the office?" she asked anxiously. Yes, she was definitely in over her head.

Annie smiled at her. "Well, you *did* lock the door."

Jordan swallowed with difficulty. She never expected that Annie would be the one to push this along. Of course, she was the one who had locked the door.

Annie's smile softened. "Don't be scared of this, Jordan."

Jordan let out her breath. "I'm terrified," she admitted.

Annie took another step closer, so close that they were almost touching. "You do remember that I'm the inexperienced one here, right?"

Jordan laughed. A nervous laugh but still a laugh. "Trust me, I have zero experience in *this* situation, Annie."

Annie took her hand and Jordan let their fingers entwine. She tightened her grip, the touch calming her nerves a little.

"Let's just take it…a day at a time," Annie said. "That's all we have to do. Take it slow, a day at a time, and see what happens."

"That simple, huh?"

Annie nodded. "That simple." She moved closer and this time, their bodies were touching. "But would you please kiss me already?"

Jordan's resolve broke and she pulled Annie impossibly close. She had no time to think, no time to decide if this was the right thing to do or not. Annie didn't give her the chance. Their lips met, and Jordan was shocked that she actually felt faint. She held on to Annie, her mouth opening slightly, taking as much as Annie would give. Annie wasn't shy and when Annie's tongue brushed hers, Jordan felt a jolt travel through her body. Her hands brought Annie's hips closer to hers, and Annie moaned in her mouth. Annie's slightly protruding belly hit Jordan's, and she realized the intimacy of their embrace. Annie's fists were grasping Jordan's shirt as their kiss deepened. She wanted so much more, but not here, not in the office.

She pulled back, both of them gasping for breath.

"My God, Jordan," Annie whispered between breaths. "Is *that* what a kiss is supposed to feel like?"

Jordan rested her forehead against Annie's as they tried to catch their breath. "We really can't do this here."

Annie nodded. "I know. Someone could need us."

Jordan laughed lightly and glanced at the sofa. "That's not really what I was thinking about."

Annie laughed too. "Really? Really, Jordan? You're going to go there?"

They pulled apart completely, both still smiling as they disengaged. Jordan noticed Annie's flushed face and wondered if hers looked the same.

Annie ran her fingers through her hair. "Okay, so what just happened here?"

"I'm not sure. I think we kissed."

Annie took a deep breath, then blew it out. "Yeah, that was some kiss." She cleared her throat. "Well, I'm certainly happy you're back."

Jordan smiled, then unlocked the door and opened it. She was glad no one was in the back room. "Yeah, me too." She shoved her hands in her pockets. "So...you get the ordering done?"

Annie moved behind the desk and sat down. "Yep. All done. No problems."

"Good."

Jordan sat on the sofa, trying to relax. So they kissed? That had been inevitable, right? The fact that she wanted to rip Annie's clothes off and make love to her wasn't really surprising either. She tapped her foot nervously, searching for a topic of conversation.

"So...lunch with Mom. You didn't say what all you talked about."

"Oh...well, we talked about you some," Annie said.

Jordan raised her eyebrows. "Why?"

Annie shrugged. "I'm not sure how it came up. We talked about when they found out you were gay."

"Oh, my God. You talked about *that*?"

Annie smiled. "You should really talk to your mom about it, Jordan. She said you have never really talked about it at all."

"What good would it do? I was twenty at the time."

Annie leaned back in her chair. "I know. We talked about Matt some too. And your mother gave me some money."

"Yeah?"

"I don't feel comfortable taking money from them."

"Annie, come on. You're carrying their grandkid. Of course they want to help."

"But still…"

"Annie, you can protest all you want, but you know they're going to help. Matt's not here to do it."

"But it's not their deal. They shouldn't have to feel obligated."

"Annie—"

"I just don't want them to think I'm taking advantage of the situation. I can provide for myself."

Jordan knew Annie treasured her independence, having had to live with her parents for so long, and she was sensitive to that.

"I know you can. But you're going to go back to school… you won't be working full time then." She met Annie's gaze. "They don't want you to struggle. I don't want you to struggle."

"Jordan, I'm living for free at your house. That's hardly struggling."

Jordan held her hand up. "You can argue all you want, Annie. It won't change the outcome."

"But I don't want—"

Annie stopped when the outer door opened. Brandon headed for the fridge, then stopped when he saw Jordan.

"Hey, boss. I didn't see you come in," he said.

"I snuck in a little while ago," she said.

"Good trip?"

She nodded. "Short and sweet. The best kind."

"Well, glad you're back. Annie's been a slave driver," he said with a laugh.

"Yeah, right," Annie said.

He got a water bottle from the fridge and went back inside the store. Jordan leaned back, then stifled a yawn. She'd been up since three that morning.

Annie looked at her questioningly. "Tired?"

"Yeah. I was up early. At the airport, you know."

"Well…maybe you should go home…take a nap."

Jordan raised her eyebrows.

Annie smiled. "Just sayin'."

Jordan met her gaze. "Should I be…scared?"

Annie winked at her. "Very scared." Then the smile left her face. "Because I'm terrified."

"Annie, you know…I would never—"

Annie held up her hand. "Jordan, I'm not terrified of *you*. I'm terrified of…*it*."

Jordan frowned. "It?"

"Yeah. *It*."

As their eyes held, Jordan finally understood what Annie was saying. "You know, *it* doesn't have to happen. Not tonight."

Annie's smile was slow and definitely sexy. "Oh, yeah, I'm pretty sure it's going to happen and soon." Annie turned in her chair, leaning closer to the sofa and Jordan. Her voice was not much more than a whisper. "You make me absolutely crazy when I'm near you. Crazy. And that's never, ever happened to me before."

Jordan felt her pulse spring to life as she recognized the look in Annie's eyes. Yes…right then, right there…she was a little afraid of *it*, too.

CHAPTER THIRTY-ONE

Annie drove home, hands gripping the steering wheel tightly. She tried not to be nervous, but she was. Would Jordan be waiting for her?

"Yeah, she's going to be naked and in bed already," she said sarcastically as she rolled her eyes.

Would they make small talk? Would they have dinner? She shook her head. No, she was far too nervous to think about eating.

But what? Would they talk about it some more? What would that accomplish other than delaying what they both wanted? Because, yes, she did want it. Her certainty of that surprised her a little. If it was a mistake, could they go back? She gripped the steering wheel even tighter, remembering their kiss. Not counting the seventh-grade smooch she'd gotten from Paul Cassel, she'd been kissed by three guys in her life—Derrick, Jason and Matt. Never once had it felt anything close to what Jordan made her feel in those few heated seconds. It couldn't possibly be a mistake.

Her mouth dropped open.

"Oh, my God," she whispered. "Am I a lesbian?"

Then she laughed. Why did that question just now surface? She was heading home with the intention of...well, of making love with another woman.

Making love? With Jordan?

She very nearly drove off the road.

* * *

Annie pulled into the carport and parked next to Jordan's SUV. She cut the engine and sat there for a few seconds, trying to get herself under control. Futile, perhaps, but she took several deep breaths. As Jordan had said, *it* didn't have to happen tonight.

The house was quiet when she went inside, and she glanced through the large windows in the living room. She found Jordan exactly where she thought she'd be—out on the deck. She wasn't sitting though. She was leaning against the railing, a wineglass within arm's reach. It was still more than an hour until sunset, but clouds to the west would obscure it this evening. She took one more deep breath, then went outside. She knew Jordan would have heard her drive up, so she wasn't surprised when Jordan didn't even turn around.

"Hey."

Jordan turned then, and Annie saw that she wasn't the only one fighting nerves. "Hey," Jordan replied.

Annie went and stood beside her, mimicking her position on the railing like she often did.

"Dinner?"

Jordan shook her head. "I didn't get anything. I wasn't sure what you'd be in the mood for."

"I'm not really hungry right now."

Jordan smiled. "That's a first."

Annie laughed, feeling some of the tension leave her. "I'm a little nervous," she admitted.

Jordan turned, facing her. She reached out a hand, letting her fingers slowly caress Annie's cheek. Annie met her gaze, seeing her brown eyes darken just a bit.

"We're going to take this slow, Annie. Give you time to... absorb what's happening."

Annie stared at her. "You think I don't know what's happening?"

"In case you decide it's not what you want." Jordan's thumb raked across her lower lip. "I don't want you to think you've jumped into something that you can't back out of."

Annie could feel her heart pounding in her chest from Jordan's gentle touch. It sounded loud in her ears, and she wondered if Jordan could hear it too. She swallowed with difficulty, finally wetting her lips where Jordan's fingers had touched.

"What if...what if you decide it's not what *you* want?" she asked. "I mean, I'm pregnant. That's probably a huge turnoff. And the fact that Matt—"

"Stop," Jordan said, putting a finger against her lips. "You're beautiful, Annie. I'm very attracted to you. The fact that you're pregnant with Matt's baby has no bearing on that." Jordan leaned closer, lightly brushing her lips against hers. "I find you beautiful inside and out. And if possible, being pregnant makes you even lovelier."

The sincerity of her words nearly melted Annie's heart. She moved nearer, into Jordan's arms. They stood close together, holding each other. She let her eyes slip closed as her arms circled Jordan's waist. There was nothing sexual about it, not this time. It was all about comfort, security, peacefulness. The stress she'd been feeling earlier vanished, and she rested against Jordan, letting Jordan's strength seep into her.

"Thank you," she murmured.

Jordan pulled back a little. "How about we drive into Fulton, go to that Italian place you like."

"Oh? You think I can eat now?"

Jordan smiled. "I don't want to face you in the morning if you go to bed without eating."

Annie playfully slapped her arm. "I am *not* that bad."

"You get cranky."

Annie took a step back. "Something with Alfredo sauce sounds good."

"Yes, it does. My treat."

She studied her for a moment. "You must be tired. You've had a long day. If you'd rather not go out, I could—"

"I'm fine," Jordan said. "I took your advice."

"A nap?"

"Yeah. A nap."

"Okay."

Annie touched her arm, waiting until Jordan's eyes met hers. She leaned closer, kissing Jordan lightly on the mouth. It was enough to send her pulse racing again.

"Just so you know," she said, "I get butterflies in my stomach when we kiss."

Jordan's eyes softened. "So do I," she whispered.

CHAPTER THIRTY-TWO

In hindsight, going out to dinner was probably a mistake. Accidental touches that weren't really accidental, lingering glances, forced small talk...the words not matching the looks in their eyes. By the time dinner was served, Annie was ready to ask for a to-go box and beg Jordan to take her back home. And not just back home. Home...to bed. But she resisted the urge and tried to enjoy the meal. She knew Jordan was fighting her own urges. So much for her gallant speech of taking things slowly.

Now, as they pulled into the driveway after a nearly silent ride home, she wondered how the night would end. It had been a silent drive, but that didn't mean they weren't communicating. Her hand had crossed the console several times to touch Jordan. She simply couldn't help it. And once, Jordan had linked their fingers, resting their hands on her thigh. Yeah, so much for taking things slow.

"I'm...I'm going to shower," she said as soon as they got inside. She needed something to distract her.

"Okay," Jordan said.

Jordan headed to the kitchen, and Annie suspected she was getting a glass of wine. Would she go out to the deck to relax? To think? To give Annie some space?

Annie didn't want space.

She took her time in the shower, trying to decide what to do. She knew it was up to her. Jordan would never push the issue, would never initiate things. No, that would be left up to Annie. When she was ready for this—mentally and physically—she would have to be the one to go to Jordan.

As she toweled off, she stared at herself in the mirror. Naked like this, it was obvious she was pregnant. Four months along now, she could no longer hide it. She touched her belly, running her hand gently across it. *A baby.* She was going to have a baby. So much change was coming. Did she really want to add to that change by…by becoming lovers with Jordan?

Lovers.

She closed her eyes, imagining just that. She was twenty-nine years old and had had only two lovers. And really, could she even count Matt? Their one time together had been brief, to say the least. But, of course, she was pregnant. She *had* to count Matt. But neither Matt nor Derrick brought her pleasure. Six years with Derrick, she could count on one hand the number of times she was able to reach an orgasm with him. At first, it never occurred to her to fake it. But it was impossible to explain to Derrick, impossible to make him understand. He simply couldn't fathom why she wasn't able to…to *get there* as easily as he did. After a while, it became easier to fake an orgasm than to go through all the drama of *not* reaching one. Toward the end of their marriage, it had gotten to the point where she could not tolerate his touch any longer. And *that* was something she refused to fake.

Was it her or was it Derrick? Was it her or was it…*men*?

She met her gaze in the mirror. Was she ready to become lovers with a woman? With Jordan? It wasn't frightened eyes that looked back at her. And she was old enough to know she had to be honest with herself. Yes, she was a little fearful about taking that step. Like Jordan had said, they couldn't go back. Once they slept together, they couldn't undo it. But something inside her, something in her soul, told her that it would be different with Jordan. She could tell that just from the few kisses they'd shared. It would be *very* different with Jordan.

She didn't see the point in delaying the inevitable any longer.

She slipped an extra-large Fat Larry T-shirt over her naked body, not bothering to put panties on. Then, with one last look in the mirror, she turned out the light and went in search of Jordan.

She heard movement in Jordan's bathroom and assumed she had finished her own shower. Should she give her some time? She took a deep breath, feeling nervous all over again. What if Jordan wasn't ready? What if Jordan really did want to take things slow?

The overhead light was off in Jordan's bedroom, but the lamp beside the bed was on. So she leaned against the doorframe to wait, remembering the looks they'd shared over dinner, remembering the tension in the car on the way back home. An electric, sexual tension that had been impossible to break. No, for all of Jordan's brave words about taking this slow, she was as ready as Annie was.

When the bathroom door opened, Annie looked up. Jordan stopped in her tracks, obviously surprised at her presence. Jordan was dressed similarly in a baggy T-shirt, her legs bare. Annie's gaze traveled up her body, stopping when she met her eyes. They were smoldering. No, Jordan didn't want to wait any longer either.

"Before you ask," she said, "yes, I'm sure."

Jordan walked over to her slowly, her eyes never breaking contact. She stopped in front of her and Annie could feel the heat between them. Jordan didn't say anything as she reached a hand out, touching Annie's face with a gentle caress. Then Jordan leaned closer, her lips barely more than a whisper as they touched her own.

When she pulled back, Jordan didn't try to hide the desire in her eyes. Annie's breath caught. Had anyone ever looked at her like that before? Like they wanted to devour her? That thought made her heart beat double-time. Yes, she wanted Jordan to devour her.

While Jordan stood mutely by, Annie took a step closer, so close that their bare legs were touching, so close that she could feel Jordan's breath on her face. Her eyes slipped closed as her mouth found Jordan's.

There was no holding back for either of them. Not any longer. Jordan's arms pulled her closer the same moment that hers slipped around Jordan's hips. She fitted herself against Jordan's body, pressing hard against her and moaning when she felt Jordan's thigh slip between hers. She pulled away from the kiss, needing to breathe, then went back again, unable to stay away. Jordan's tongue drew hers inside Jordan's mouth, causing her knees to threaten to buckle. She grasped Jordan's hips, steadying herself as their kiss came to an end.

The kiss came to an end, but Jordan didn't release her hold on Annie. Annie could hear Jordan's thundering heartbeat against her ear as she tried to catch her breath. Then soft lips were moving across her face, down to her neck, nibbling gently against her skin. Those lips moved to her ear, and she moaned again when a wet tongue bathed it.

Annie could barely decipher Jordan's whispered words in her heated state. "Make love." *Yes.* "Bed." *Yes.*

She stood still as Jordan reached for her shirt, silently asking if she could remove it. Annie met her gaze, nodding ever so slightly. It was with agonizing slowness that Jordan lifted the bottom, pulling it slowly up and over her head.

"Jesus, Annie," Jordan said, her voice husky with desire. "You're so beautiful."

Annie felt beautiful at that moment as Jordan's gaze swept across her body, landing finally on her breasts. Annie could hear Jordan's uneven breathing, matching her own quick breaths. She was surprised to see Jordan's hand tremble as she reached out to touch her.

Warm hands slid up her body, stopping under her breasts. Again, Jordan seemed to be asking permission. Annie covered

Jordan's hands with her own, then slid them higher, over her breasts, unable to prevent a moan from escaping when Jordan touched her there for the first time. Her eyes slammed shut when Jordan rubbed both nipples with her thumbs, turning them rock-hard. She felt a jolt to her very core and thought crazily that she might be about to have an orgasm, just from that little stimulation.

Fearing she might actually fall down, she held on tightly to Jordan as her mouth was again claimed in a fiery kiss. It was all almost too much…an overload on her senses. Jordan must have suspected as much for she ended the kiss and moved toward the bed.

Jordan unceremoniously tossed the covers back, then just as quickly shed her own T-shirt, leaving her as naked as Annie was. She drew Annie down on the bed and Annie reached for her immediately, pulling Jordan to her. No longer having to fear that her legs would fail her, she opened to Jordan, their legs scissoring between each other's. As Jordan's thigh pressed against her center, she knew without a doubt that she'd never— ever—been more aroused. She could feel her own wetness, and she jerked hard against Jordan when Jordan's mouth settled over her breast, her tongue gentle washing her rigid nipple.

"I think I'm going to pass out," she murmured as her head rolled from side to side on the pillow.

Jordan's lips nibbled at her neck, then moved to her mouth, kissing her slowly, with purpose.

"Should we slow down?" Jordan whispered against her mouth.

"Or hurry up," she countered.

She matched Jordan's smile against her lips, then moaned with satisfaction as those lips returned to her breast.

Jordan nudged her legs apart, and Annie gave her room, sighing with pleasure as Jordan settled against her. Annie didn't know what she expected their lovemaking to be like. She'd been afraid to even speculate on it for very long, for the thought of being with Jordan—like this—caused her insides to become all jumbled up. But for what she did imagine, she didn't expect it to be so…so slow, so measured. She hadn't anticipated Jordan being so thorough as her lips moved across her skin, leaving little untouched by them.

As Jordan's hips began to roll against her, Annie opened wider, straining to touch her. She felt Jordan's wetness against her thigh and she so wanted to touch her, to feel that wetness with her fingers.

She didn't voice her desire, she simply…*did*. Her gasp mingled with Jordan's as her hand moved between them. It was like liquid fire as her fingers probed deeper, exploring a place that was foreign, yet familiar. She didn't have time to reflect on that thought, however. Jordan shifted, giving her more room and her fingers slipped inside her as if she'd done this very thing a hundred times before.

"Jesus…Annie," Jordan breathed, her hips rocking against her fingers.

"I don't know what I'm doing."

Jordan's hips slowed, finally stopping, but Annie's fingers remained inside her. Their eyes met, and Annie was shocked by the fire she saw in Jordan's.

"I'm going to go inside you too," Jordan whispered.

Annie held on to Jordan's gaze, only losing it when her eyes slammed closed. Jordan's fingers brushed her clit, then moved inside her. Annie gasped for breath as her hips arched up, letting Jordan fill her.

"Sweet Jesus," Annie murmured.

"You're so wet." Jordan's fingers moved inside her. "I'm not hurting you, am I?"

"God, no," Annie said as her hips began to move, matching the rhythm Jordan set.

She was aware of Jordan moving against her hand, aware of her fingers inside Jordan, aware of Jordan inside her. But that awareness faded into the background with each stroke of Jordan's thumb against her clit. Her heartbeat became a roar in her ears and she struggled to breathe. Feelings completely alien to her assaulted her senses, leaving no room for contemplation.

For the first time in her life, she was completely overwhelmed by her orgasm. It hit with such dizzying speed that she had no time to prepare, no time to…to anticipate it. Her world exploded in an array of colors more beautiful than any painter could have contrived. A scream of pleasure burst from her mouth so quickly, she couldn't even attempt to contain it.

Then Jordan thrust harder against her hand and Annie forced herself to focus on Jordan. It only took a few seconds, and she watched in amazement as Jordan's expression changed, her eyes squeezed shut, her mouth drawing in quick breaths. Then she seemed to still, to hold her breath, then finally let it out with a loud moan, her pleasure evident on her face.

Annie relaxed finally, feeling Jordan nearly collapse on top of her. She withdrew her fingers from Jordan's wetness, then moved her hands across Jordan's back, pulling her even closer.

They lay together like that for a few minutes, long enough for their breathing to return somewhat to normal. Then Jordan moved, rolling over to her side. Annie shifted too, turning so she could see Jordan's eyes.

"That was…well, I want to say fabulous, but that doesn't even begin to describe how I feel," she said.

Jordan lifted her hand, her fingers tracing Annie's nipple lightly. Annie stilled Jordan's hand, instead, she reached out, touching Jordan's breast for the first time. She was so soft, her skin smooth, her nipple rigid. Annie's fingers rubbed against the nipple, and she watched as it hardened even more. She looked up, meeting Jordan's gaze.

"You're so soft," she murmured. "It feels good to touch you."

Jordan leaned closer, kissing her softly on the mouth. "You're a very quick learner."

Annie smiled. "I think I'm going to need *lots* of practice though."

CHAPTER THIRTY-THREE

Jordan stared at the office laptop, trying to remember what she was doing. She shook her head, finally closing it. She'd been trying to get something accomplished for the last hour, yet she could not concentrate on anything. Her mind was still filled with Annie and their night—and morning—together.

When was the last time she'd had a lover who was so in sync with her? Ever? Debra had been the most frequent lover she'd had, and even though the sex had been great between them, they'd never been quite as in tune as she and Annie had been last night.

And to think that Annie had never been with a woman before. The night had simply been incredible. Jordan's very long day had caught up with her and she'd collapsed finally, sleep claiming her instantly. But she'd woken up at four, still tangled together with Annie. She'd tried to move, to roll over. The lamp was still on and she was reaching for it, intending to turn it off. Annie's eyes had opened, sleepy and sated, yet they were shimmering in desire. Jordan had been helpless to refuse.

She'd rolled to her back, pulling Annie on top of her. Annie had surprised her yet again as she'd moved down her body, her mouth and lips missing little on their journey.

Jordan blew out her breath as she remembered Annie's face buried between her legs, her mouth and tongue driving her mad. For having no experience, Annie hadn't shied away from anything. Jordan had been embarrassed by the scream that nearly choked her when she climaxed. Then Annie's mouth and lips made a return journey up her body, stopping only when they reached her mouth, kissing her with such an agonizing passion that Jordan nearly climaxed again.

"I think I'm in big trouble," she murmured.

She got up from the chair and walked out to get another cup of coffee, anything to occupy her mind and keep memories of last night away.

What was Annie thinking this morning? Jordan had crawled out of bed at seven, and Annie hadn't even budged. She'd showered and dressed, finding Annie still curled on her side, sound asleep. She decided not to wake her. She didn't bother with coffee or breakfast. She picked up both on her way to Fat Larry's.

And now here she was, nervously awaiting Annie's arrival. Would it be awkward to see her in the light of day? Would Annie be sorry they'd slept together? Would she want to talk? Discuss it?

With a shake of her head, Jordan went back into the office. Whatever Annie wanted, whatever she needed, Jordan would have to go with it. And if Annie thought it was a huge mistake, then they would just have to live with it.

If that turned out to be the case, it would certainly make leaving that much easier. Hell, if that was the case, she might head out earlier than September. No sense hanging around if there was going to be tension between them.

Her head was spinning with so many unanswered questions, so many scenarios running through her mind. She had to stop or she would drive herself crazy until Annie got there. Fortunately, she didn't have to wait any longer. The outer door opened and she glanced up, finding Annie staring back at her. She was relieved by the smile Annie gave her. She returned it, her fears slipping away.

"You're late," she said as Annie walked into the office.

"Yeah...about that," Annie said. "I hope my boss will cut me some slack. I kinda had a rather...well, a rather *eventful* night."

"Oh, yeah?" Jordan felt her face turn red.

Annie laughed. "You're so cute when you blush."

Jordan blushed even more. "So...do we need to talk?"

Annie tilted her head. "No. I'm good." She arched an eyebrow. "You?"

Jordan flashed a grin, her relief obvious. "Oh, yeah. I'm good."

Annie's slow smile caused Jordan to stop breathing entirely. "Yes...you are definitely...*good.*"

* * *

Annie folded up a T-shirt, placing it neatly back in its bin. She found herself singing along to a Lady Gaga song. She smiled when she realized what she was doing. While Jordan allowed most of Matt's old classics to play, she'd added some songs "from this century" to the mix.

She glanced up as the bell chimed and she smiled at the two customers who had walked in. For a Sunday, they had been busy, and Molly had volunteered to work the afternoon as well as the morning. Normally, she and Jordan handled the Sunday duties by themselves, with one of the others working a short ten-to-two shift. When two o'clock came and the store had been crowded, Molly offered to stay, saying she had no plans for the afternoon. Annie thought Molly had really grown over the summer. She was much more interactive with the customers now and showed none of the shyness that she'd first exhibited. She hoped that carried over to her senior year of high school.

She sighed. School. Yes, her last year of college would be starting soon too. To say the summer had flown by was an understatement. It seemed like only yesterday that they were having Matt's funeral, that she'd first met Jordan. And it seemed like only weeks ago—not months—that she'd found out she was pregnant. Yet, in three short weeks, she'd be starting classes again.

And in three short weeks, Jordan would be making plans to leave, to go back to Chicago. Annie felt a tightness in her chest that was nearly painful. Jordan was going to leave soon.

She wasn't ready for Jordan to leave. Not now. Not now that they were...lovers.

She closed her eyes for a second. *Lovers.* Yes, they were definitely lovers. Images from last night flashed through her mind in record speed, causing her heart to race. What she'd had in the past with Derrick, with Matt, couldn't even begin to compare to the intimacy of what she'd shared with Jordan last night. Making love took on an entirely new meaning with Jordan.

"Hey."

She turned, finding Jordan watching her. She cleared her throat. "Hey."

Jordan walked closer and Annie felt the heat between them. She thought perhaps Jordan could read her mind, for when their eyes met, she saw a shimmer of desire in Jordan's.

"My mother called. She's making lasagna. She wanted to know if we wanted to stop by the house on our way home."

Annie nodded, even though what she really wanted to do was to head straight home and have a repeat of last night. "Sure." Then she smiled. "You know I'll never pass up a meal," she said as she patted her stomach.

Jordan laughed. "Okay, I'll let her know." Her gaze drifted across the store. "Why are we so busy today?"

"School starts soon. A lot of people are taking their last vacations of the summer," she said. "And you should not be complaining about being busy."

"I know." She paused. "I can't stop thinking about last night."

Annie reached out and squeezed Jordan's hand quickly before releasing it. "Me either."

Jordan's eyes darkened. "I vote we decline the dinner invitation."

Annie felt the now-familiar flutter of butterflies in her stomach. "Good. Gets my vote too."

CHAPTER THIRTY-FOUR

Jordan leaned on her elbow, watching Annie sleep. Once again, the lamp had been forgotten and the bedroom was still bathed in a soft glow. Her hand was resting against Annie's belly...against the baby. She kept still, hoping to feel the baby move, even though it was probably too early. Annie said her doctor told her it would be another few weeks before she felt movement. That thought made her sad. In a few weeks she would be leaving, heading back to her life in Chicago. She knew it would be hard to leave, but now that they were lovers, it would be doubly so.

Annie stirred and Jordan watched as her eyes fluttered open, then closed again. A smile on Annie's lips told her she was awake.

"I guess we fell asleep," Annie mumbled. She turned her head, her eyes opening again. "Or I did."

"Me too."

Annie rolled over, facing her. Under the covers, her hand moved to Jordan's breasts, stroking one lightly.

"What are you thinking about?"

Jordan met her gaze. "Nothing, really," she lied. "I was hoping to feel the baby move."

Annie took Jordan's hand and pressed it against her belly. "The doctor said that since it's my first baby, I probably wouldn't feel it until about twenty weeks or more. I'm at seventeen now."

Jordan sank lower under the covers and pulled Annie flush against her. "So...what do you want? Boy or girl?"

Annie smiled. "I don't know. I think a little boy would be fun. I'm not really into dress-up. Suzanne and Macy both have girls. Macy has two. All the bows and crap they make them wear...I can't see me doing that."

Jordan laughed quietly. "So jeans and a Fat Larry T-shirt on the little man and you're good to go?"

"Wouldn't that be cute?"

"Yeah, that would be adorable." Her smile faltered somewhat. She wondered if she'd be around to see it.

"What?"

Jordan raised her eyebrows.

Annie pulled her hand from under the covers and cupped Jordan's face, her fingers playing gently against her skin. "Do we need to talk?"

Jordan sighed. "I'll be leaving soon."

Annie's hand stilled. "I don't like to think about you leaving."

"The time...well, it kinda got away from me. I was supposed to hire someone to run the store when I leave. And you'll be starting school again pretty soon."

"I'm going to still work part-time," Annie said. "And if Brandon could take some more hours, I think we can manage it."

"I know the winters aren't that busy, but maybe Molly would work Saturdays." She rolled over onto her back and folded one arm behind her head. "I'm not ready to leave, Annie."

Annie rested her head on Jordan's shoulder, snuggling closer. "I don't want you to leave either."

Jordan sighed again, wondering why she was trying so hard to convince herself leaving was the right thing to do. "I have to. I own a condo. My job...I worked so hard to get where I am.

Peter is expecting me by September. I don't think he'll hold my job after that."

Annie curled her arm around Jordan's waist. "You're going to come back though, right? You're not going to disappear, are you? Because I kinda need you here."

Jordan could hear the panic in Annie's voice. She rolled to her side again, facing Annie. She kissed her slowly, her lips fitting between Annie's. "I'm not going to disappear," she whispered. "I promise."

CHAPTER THIRTY-FIVE

Annie had just finished with a customer when a familiar face walked into the store. Her mother in Fat Larry's was the last thing she expected.

"Shopping?" she asked.

Her mother shook her head. "I thought maybe you would have time for lunch."

Annie's eyebrows shot up. "Lunch? That's a first."

"Well, it's been a while since you've been by the house. Or called, for that matter."

Annie put her hands on her hips. "Really, Mom? You expect me to continue begging you for acceptance? The last time I called, you were too busy for me. Remember?"

"Yes, I remember. I'm sorry," she said. Her mother's gaze swept over her. "You look…really good, Annie."

Annie smiled. "Thank you. I feel good."

"So? Lunch? Can you take a break?"

"Sure. Let me tell Jordan. I'll be right back."

Annie found Jordan in the office, a smile on her face. She looked up when Annie walked in, and she pointed to the monitor.

"Look at this," Jordan said. "Even though we give away Fat Larry T-shirts all the time, they're still one of our top sellers. Especially the new design with Fat Larry sunning on the beach. Crazy."

"Do I need to remind you who thought of that design?"

Jordan laughed. "No, you don't."

Annie touched her shoulder lightly. "It seems I have a lunch date," she said.

"Oh, yeah?"

"My mother came in. Invited me to have lunch with her."

Jordan nodded. "That's good, right?"

"I guess. As long as she doesn't launch into one of her speeches about how horrible it is to be an unwed mother. Or bring up me and Derrick getting back together."

"Well, then go to lunch across the street at Pepe's. That way, if she starts in on you, you can get up and leave," Jordan suggested.

Annie smiled. "Good idea. I *am* craving Mexican food, after all." She raised an eyebrow. "Want me to bring something back for you?"

"Yeah. The chicken enchilada platter would be good." Jordan stood up and pulled some money from her pocket.

"I can get it," Annie offered.

But Jordan placed the money in her palm anyway. "No need. You're about to become a college student again."

"Don't remind me," she said. "Because that means you'll be leaving."

Jordan's smile faded. "I thought we weren't going to talk about it."

"I know." She plastered a smile on her face. "I better get going. See you in a bit."

"Have fun."

Annie paused at the door, then turned around. "If I tell you something, will you promise me you won't freak out?"

Jordan shrugged. "Okay. I don't freak out too easily."

Annie met her gaze across the room. "I just...well...I thought you should know that I'm falling in love with you."

She turned on her heels before Jordan could respond and hurried out the door. God, it felt good to say that. Scary, but good. Because last night when they made love, she could almost feel Jordan taking ahold of her heart. She had felt a swelling of emotions that she'd never experienced before. Surely this is what falling in love feels like.

But should she have told Jordan? God, what if Jordan…what if she wasn't feeling *any* of these same emotions? Was she being presumptuous to assume that Jordan was falling in love too? She very nearly panicked. She should go to Jordan, take back her words. Tell Jordan her hormones were all jacked up again.

"Oh, God, you're so stupid," she murmured.

But the sight of her mother stopped her from going back into the office. She took a deep breath, trying to settle her nerves. So she told Jordan she was falling in love? They would deal with it just like they'd done everything else. It would be fine. *She* would be fine. And maybe it was her hormones. Who knows?

"All set?" her mother asked.

Annie nodded. "I'm craving Mexican food," she said. "How about across the street at Pepe's?"

"That's fine. I haven't been there recently."

"I eat there quite a bit," Annie said as she held the door open for her mother. "Or else Jordan picks up something and we eat in the office."

"You live together, you work together *and* you eat together? You must be sick of each other's company by now."

Wow. They hadn't even made it across the street yet and her mother was already starting. Annie decided she wasn't in the mood to argue with her today.

"We get along great, thanks." When they got to Pepe's, she again held the door open for her mother. "And we don't always work together. Jordan comes and goes, especially since Brandon can close now." She smiled at Emily and held up two fingers, then turned back to her mother. "How is Dad?"

"Fine. He misses you. We both do."

"Funny. He hasn't called me once." She smiled quickly. "Neither have you."

Emily came up. "How's a booth today, Annie?"

"Great. Thank you."

They followed her to their table and sat down. Emily didn't even bother to place a menu in front of her, only giving one to her mother. A basket of chips and two small bowls of salsa were brought out and Annie reached for a chip immediately.

"No menu?" her mother asked.

"I get the same thing every time," she said. "Chicken enchiladas with sour cream sauce."

"Sounds good. I may try that too."

Annie loaded a chip with salsa, nearly moaning at the taste. While she'd always enjoyed Mexican food, her sudden craving for hot and spicy food was a bit odd for her. Thankfully, she had no adverse effects from it and ate it at will.

"So I guess you've been to the doctor a couple of times now, right?"

"Yes."

"And when are you due?"

"January fifteenth," she said.

"That will be here before you know it."

"I know. I'm told the last couple of months are the longest," she said.

"So have you told everyone?"

Annie smiled. "It's not like I can hide it any longer," she said, motioning to the blouse she was wearing. "Suzanne went shopping with me, since you were too busy to go," she said. "I didn't get a lot though. I can't believe how expensive maternity clothes are."

Her mother ignored the jab at her. "Well, you look beautiful, Annie. Happy. Radiant, in fact."

Annie felt a blush on her face. She wondered if her sudden radiance was due to being pregnant or to having the best sex she'd ever had in her life.

"I feel good," she said. "My morning sickness stopped, thankfully. I'd read horror stories of women being sick for months during pregnancy."

"I only had a touch of it myself," her mother said. "You don't look like you've gained weight. I hardly gained any when I was pregnant with you."

"I feel fat and I eat like a pig," she said with a laugh. "Jordan assures me that I'm *not* fat, however." She looked up as Emily came back over.

"Ready to order? I'm assuming you'll have your usual?"

"Yep. And my mother will have the same. Two teas."

"Okay. It'll be right out."

"Oh, Emily. And I need an order to go."

"For Jordan? The usual? Extra rice, no beans?"

"Yes, thanks."

"I guess you must come here a lot if they know what you order each time," her mother said.

"At least once a week, sometimes twice," she said. "Either that or Subway. I get a turkey sandwich with mounds of banana peppers on it. I don't know why I've been craving peppers and spicy food."

"Everyone craves different things, I guess. I was predictable and ate a jar of dill pickles nearly every day."

"So far, no pickle cravings," she said.

Her mother folded her hands together, a gesture Annie knew signaled an end to their small talk.

"We want you to move back home with us."

Annie frowned. "Why?"

"You need to be with your family, that's why."

Annie leaned forward, eyebrows raised. "What about all of your worries? What will the neighbors say? What about your friends at church? What about all that?"

"I was…in shock, Annie. You, of all people, getting pregnant? I handled it poorly, I know."

"Poorly is an understatement, Mom. You turned your back on me," she said bluntly.

"That's not true. I asked you not to move out. I asked you to stay."

Annie shook her head. "I'm not going to argue with you. And thank you for the offer. But no."

"No? Why not? You'll need some help, Annie. Once this baby is born, you'll need my help."

"And you'll be welcome to come out to Pelican's Landing to help, if you'd like. I know Loraine will be there."

"Pelican's Landing?"

"The house on the bay. Where I live," she said. "Surely you saw the sign when you came over for dinner."

"Who names their house?"

Annie smiled. "Jordan said her grandmother named it before the house was even built. The pier apparently attracted pelicans. It still does."

"And Loraine? Mrs. Sims?"

"Yes. She's offered to help. In fact, she gave me some money for new clothes," she said.

"Are you already running low on money? The baby's not even born yet, Annie. What will you do when—"

"Stop," she said, holding up her hand. "I'm not low on money. She offered to help, is all. She's very nice."

"Well, considering it was her son that got you into this mess, I would hope so."

"Mess? I suppose you could look at it like that." Annie shrugged. "I'm actually getting kinda excited. I don't see it as a mess."

"You know what I mean."

Annie was thankful their lunch arrived, saving her from commenting. Really, her mother was too much for her to deal with.

"This looks good."

Annie nodded and shoved a forkful into her mouth. The sour cream and cheese melted in her mouth and she moaned with pleasure. Yes, she could eat this every day.

"Annie, will you at least consider moving back with us? Please?"

"Why, Mom? I love where I am. It feels like home to me now."

"You are living with a…*lesbian*," her mother spat. "Do you not care what people are going to say about you?"

"Oh, God…are we back to that again? First of all, who is going to say anything about me? People from your church? How would they even know about Jordan?"

"Rockport is not a big town, Annie. Of course people know. Her parents are as well known as anyone in town. You think people don't know about their daughter?" Her mother leaned closer. "I heard that was the reason she never comes back here. Because her parents don't want her around. They're afraid it'll affect their business."

"Gossiping, are you?"

Her mother had the grace to blush. "I simply overheard someone talking."

"Right." The enchiladas were so good. Too bad she'd lost her appetite. She put her fork down. "Listen, I don't care what people say about me. They don't know me. They don't know Jordan. I'm happy there, Mom. I'm almost thirty years old. I have no business living at your house."

"You have no business living with that woman."

Annie met her gaze. "What are you afraid of, Mom?"

"I just think it would be best for all concerned if you moved back home."

"You mean, best for you," Annie said. "Look, I want you in my life, Mom. I want you there when this baby is born. I want you involved in that. But I will not put up with your constant badgering over it. Jordan is…she's there for me, Mom. No matter what, she's there. I trust her with my life. And her parents are going to be there for me too," she said. "So I really, really wish you'd get over this already. Because I want you there for me too."

Her mother stared at her. "It's like you're throwing your life away. Why, when Derrick came to see you—"

"I was wondering how long it would be before you brought Derrick's name up." Annie pointed her finger at her mother. "It's none of your business, Mom. Derrick and I talked. He knows we're not ever getting back together. I'd hoped he had passed that on to you."

"He's a *good* man, Annie. You need—"

"I don't love him," she said. "Don't you know that by now? Why would I go back to a man I don't love?"

"Security, for one."

"I'm sorry, but my happiness means more to me than that." She held a hand up and waved at Emily. "A to-go box, please."

Her mother looked at her plate. "You're not eating?"

"I've lost my appetite."

"And I suppose you blame that on me."

Annie laughed. "You're too much."

"No, *you're* too much," her mother said. "You won't even try."

"Try what? What are we talking about now? Try with Derrick? Try moving back with you? Try getting *along* with you? What?"

Her mother reached across the table and took her hand. "Annie, where did we go wrong?"

Annie rolled her eyes. "Really? That's your next move?" She pulled her hand away. All of this drama because she was pregnant? She cringed, imagining what her mother's reaction would be if she knew she and Jordan were sleeping together.

"It's like you don't care, Annie. You don't care about us."

"Do you hear what you're saying? Because I'll say it back to you. It's like you don't care, Mom. You don't care about *me*."

"Nonsense."

Annie held her hand up. "This is getting us nowhere." She gave a relieved sigh when Emily brought over Jordan's lunch bag and her to-go box. "Thanks," she said, quickly scraping her mostly uneaten meal into the container.

"So you're leaving?"

"I can't possibly take another minute of this very enjoyable lunch," she said sarcastically. "Thank you so much. It's always a pleasure when we have these talks."

"So you're going to walk away? We haven't solved anything."

Annie stood and tossed the money Jordan had given her onto the table. "I wasn't aware there was anything to solve. I'm happy. You said so yourself. You said I looked happy, I looked radiant." She bent down, looking her mother in the eye. "So let me *be* happy. Please."

She turned and left her mother sitting there, not realizing she was shaking until she was outside. She headed across the street to the store, wishing now that she'd not blurted out her feelings to Jordan. Because right now, she really, really needed a hug from her. The last thing she wanted to do was to talk.

She nodded at Staci as she walked to the back and pushed the door open. She glanced toward the office, seeing Jordan sitting behind the desk. Jordan met her gaze as she entered.

Annie put the food on the desk, then turned around and closed the door. When she turned back around, Jordan was watching her.

"About what I said earlier," she said. "Can we forget about that for now?"

Jordan stood and came closer. "What did she say to you?"

Annie felt tears in her eyes. "What *didn't* she say?"

Jordan pulled her close and Annie sank into her embrace, burying her face against Jordan's neck.

"It'll be okay," Jordan said.

"Yes. You always make it okay, don't you?"

"I try."

Annie squeezed her eyes shut, her mother's words fading from her mind. She was in Jordan's arms, feeling safe and secure. Feeling...loved.

CHAPTER THIRTY-SIX

"I thought you should know I'm falling in love with you."

The words reverberated over and over in Jordan's mind. She didn't know why she was shocked that Annie had uttered them. Throughout this whole…affair of theirs, Annie had not shied away from one single part of it. In fact, she seemed even more confident than Jordan did.

Jordan walked down the steps of the deck and out to the pier. It was wider than the old one and much sturdier. She made her way down to the end and sat on the bench. It was a hot afternoon, the sun blazing down, but the breeze on the bay brought some relief. There were no pelicans out, no gulls. Low tide and the water lapped lazily against the pylons. If not for the breeze, it would be quiet and still, something she would never associate with the constant movement of the bay.

She stared out over the water, absently watching the shimmering ripples as the sun splashed off it. Annie was falling in love with her. She leaned her head against the post and looked skyward. At least Annie recognized it. At least it wouldn't be a total shock to her when Jordan told her the same thing.

Because as each day passed, each night, she fell a little more…fell a little harder, fell a little deeper. She was falling in love and she could do nothing to stop it. She didn't *want* to stop it. It felt too good. But then what?

She was leaving in two weeks. What would happen then? Would they talk on the phone each day? Would she come back a couple of times a month? Would that be enough?

No, she didn't think so. Their relationship was new, it was still fragile. How could they possibly maintain it…nourish it when they would be living apart?

"I don't want to leave," she whispered, the breeze carrying her words away.

No, she didn't want to leave Annie. Hell, she'd known that when Peter had called and whisked her back to Chicago…and she and Annie weren't even lovers then. She shook her head. How had this happened? How could her life turn upside down so quickly? She loved her job. She loved her freedom and independence. She even loved Chicago.

Right, she thought dryly. Concrete and steel. Brutally long, cold winters. Yeah, she couldn't *wait* to get back to that.

She saw movement out of the corner of her eye and turned, finding Annie walking toward her. She couldn't stop the smile that touched her face. No matter the turmoil in her mind, Annie's presence chased it all away.

"You mind company?"

"No. Come sit."

Annie sat down on the bench beside her and stretched her legs out. "It's hot."

"Yeah, a little." She met her gaze. "You feeling better?"

Annie nodded. "Yeah. Thanks. Remind me to decline any future invitations from my mother."

"I still say we should have them over with my parents. It might help if she sees how my mother treats you."

Annie shrugged. "We'll see. I might pass it by your mom."

"Oh?"

Annie nodded. "She's going with me to my doctor's appointment tomorrow, remember."

"That's right. A trip to the mall is in your future."

Annie leaned closer, letting their shoulders touch. "So…you ready to talk about it?"

Jordan smiled. No, Annie didn't shy away from anything. She met it all head-on. Jordan took her hand, letting their fingers entwine.

"There's nothing to talk about, Annie." Jordan waited until Annie looked at her questioningly. "I'm falling in love with you too," she said simply.

Annie held her gaze, and Jordan felt as if Annie were reaching inside her very soul to touch her. Annie, very slowly, leaned closer. Their kiss was light, gentle, brief. But it was enough to convey what they both were feeling.

"Let's go inside," Annie suggested. "Where it's cool." She paused, meeting Jordan's eyes again. "I want to make love."

* * *

Annie moved down Jordan's body, her lips kissing every inch of her. Would she ever tire of loving her this way? She loved the unique smell and taste of Jordan, loved the quiet sounds Jordan made as she nibbled against her skin. Loved the power she had as she made love to Jordan with her mouth.

She spread Jordan's thighs, inhaling deeply, the musky scent of Jordan's arousal stirring her own senses, causing her to push Jordan's legs apart even further. She moaned with pleasure as she found Jordan's clit with her tongue, her hands trying to hold Jordan still on the bed. It was to no avail as Jordan's hips rocked against her face and her fingers threaded their way into her hair.

Her mouth covered Jordan's clit entirely, sucking it hard inside her mouth. Jordan jerked up, her fingers tightening in Annie's hair.

"God…Annie…so good," Jordan breathed.

Yes. So good. Annie lost herself in giving pleasure to Jordan. Her eyes closed as she continued to flick her tongue back and forth against Jordan's clit. Time ceased to exist. She had no idea if mere seconds or minutes had passed when she felt Jordan's thighs clamp around her face, her hips arching one last time before she cried out. The fingers in her hair clutched her almost painfully as Jordan climaxed. Annie felt Jordan tremble against her mouth and very nearly had her own orgasm. Then Jordan stilled, fingers slipping away, her hands resting limply on the bed. Annie finally pulled her mouth from Jordan, crawling up her body, her lips kissing damp skin, pausing at her breasts.

No, she would never tire of this.

"Have I told you what a quick learner you are?"

Annie smiled as her tongue raked across Jordan's nipple. "I believe you might have mentioned that once or twice."

"Come here."

Annie let Jordan pull her up, into her arms. She snuggled against her, her lips now nibbling aimlessly across Jordan's neck.

"Have I told you how much I love being with you like this?"

She heard Jordan's quiet laugh. "I believe you might have mentioned that once or twice."

Annie raised her head, kissing Jordan on the mouth. "I want to do it again," she whispered.

But Jordan rolled them over. "No. My turn."

Annie had no time to protest as Jordan moved down her body. She spread her legs willingly, gasping as Jordan's tongue snaked through her wetness. Her eyes slipped closed, and time once again ceased to exist as Jordan made love to her.

CHAPTER THIRTY-SEVEN

Annie yawned, then glanced over at Loraine apologetically. "Sorry."

"Are you not sleeping well?"

Annie felt herself blush, and she turned to look out the window, hoping Loraine didn't notice. "I'm sleeping fine," she said.

When they took time to sleep, that is. God, what an awesome night it had been. She had been positively insatiable, her hands and mouth going to Jordan time and again. She lost count how many times they'd loved each other. Sleep was intermittent at best.

"I slept fitfully during my pregnancy with Jordan," Loraine said. "Completely different with Matt. If I got two hours with Jordan, I was happy. With Matt, I could sleep nine or ten hours," she said with a laugh. "Maybe I was making up for lost sleep with Jordan."

Annie glanced over at her. "I normally sleep very well," she said.

Loraine nodded, then turned her attention back to the road. She had offered to drive and Annie had been thankful. She doubted she'd had more than three hours sleep. Jordan had already been gone when her alarm woke her. She didn't remember setting it on her phone and thought Jordan must have done it for her. She had to force herself to get up and shower when all she wanted to do was roll over and go back to sleep. By the time Loraine had shown up, she'd barely made it through her first cup of coffee.

"Jordan mentioned that you had lunch with your mother."

Annie nodded. "And did she mention how it went?"

"I'm sorry, Annie. I don't know what your mother is thinking."

"For one, she's embarrassed by my pregnancy," she said. "I mean, that I'm not married. She's very traditional that way."

"That still doesn't excuse how she treats you."

"I know. I keep thinking she'll come around. Her big thing right now is that she wants me to move back home with them."

Loraine nodded. "Because of Jordan."

Annie turned in her seat, facing Loraine. "She's afraid people are going to start…talking about us," she said, making quotation marks with her fingers. "People in her church."

"You and Jordan?"

"Yes."

Loraine shook her head. "You would think that people would have more important things to worry about than that." She glanced at her. "Or is that what your mother is really worried about? That you and Jordan are…more than friends?"

Annie met her gaze, wondering if Loraine suspected how far their relationship had evolved. She nodded.

"Yes. I think the fact that Jordan is gay is the root of her problem. When I first moved in with Jordan, that was her main objection."

Loraine smiled. "Well, as far as I know, *gay* isn't contagious. You either are or you're not."

Annie nodded again, then turned her gaze out the window, afraid to look at Loraine. *You either are or you're not.* Yes, it should be that simple. But was it? Annie thought back over the years, back to high school. Before that, even. She had innocent crushes on boys, just like her friends did. She was in the ninth grade when Derrick started paying her attention. They hung out after school, they went to the movies together, they went to football games on Friday nights. And they went parking and made out. It was what everyone else was doing. Her world was small, and she never wondered what it would be like with someone other than Derrick. Not until she was older and already married did she question it. Even then, she never once considered she might be gay. She just assumed she hadn't met the right guy yet. Little did she know, she was waiting to meet the right *woman*.

A hand on her arm startled her and she turned, finding Loraine watching her.

"If you need to talk, I'm a good listener," Loraine offered.

Annie met her eyes, seeing a gentleness there that reminded her of Jordan. She realized that Jordan must get her compassion from her mother. Annie smiled quickly.

"You know, don't you?"

Loraine squeezed her arm, then put her hand back on the steering wheel. "They say women have a radiance about them when they're pregnant. But I say it's because they're in love." She looked at Annie. "Why else would both you *and* Jordan be glowing?"

"Oh, God…you *do* know."

Loraine smiled. "I suspected, yes." She held her hand up. "And it's absolutely none of my business. You're both adults."

Annie clutched her hands together nervously. "I think maybe it is your business," she said. "Because I'm pregnant with Matt's baby." She turned toward her. "I should explain. Truthfully. I should tell you exactly what happened."

"Annie, I'm not judging you."

"Thank you. But you deserve to know." She smiled. "You did say you were a good listener," she reminded her.

"So I did."

Annie swallowed. "Jordan and I…well, we have this connection between us. Ever since the day we first met, we've had it. And it's come to this. All summer, we got closer and closer and now...now we're lovers." She met Loraine's gaze. "And it feels so good to say that out loud." She tilted her head, watching her drive. "Please don't think poorly of me...or more importantly, Jordan."

"I don't, Annie. I love my daughter. I won't interfere in her personal life."

"I guess you don't know my history. I married right out of high school—Derrick—dated him all through school and got married. I knew it was a mistake right away. I wasn't in love with him. I wasn't attracted to him. Yet I stayed married to him for six years. I didn't want to have sex with him. I didn't want to sleep with him." She turned her gaze away from her, knowing how this made her sound. "I know what you're thinking. If I didn't love him, why did I get married?"

"I was eighteen once too, you know."

Annie laughed. "Yeah, I blame it on my age. My mother adored Derrick. There was never a dissenting voice to be heard."

"It took you six years to work up the courage to leave?"

"Yes. I kept thinking something was wrong with me and that I would change. But after I divorced, I never wanted to be with anyone...like that. I wasn't interested in dating, I wasn't interested in sex. I wasn't attracted to anyone."

"Not even Matt?"

Annie shook her head. "I'm sorry. No."

"Then how—"

"It was a rainy night and I didn't want to go home to my parents. I was...so lonely." She thought back to that night, remembering how desperate she'd been for someone's touch, anyone's touch. "Matt, he flirted with me all the time, always teasing with me. And that night, I gave in to it because...well, because I thought something was wrong with me. I had no desire for anyone, nothing. I thought surely something was wrong and if I just...*did it*, maybe it would be all right." She paused. "And I got pregnant. That was the result of that one night." She leaned her head back. "Now Jordan...she's turned my world upside down. I've never...I've never felt like this before." She glanced over at Loraine. "A part of me is so afraid though. She makes me feel things I only dreamed of feeling." She took a deep breath. "So please don't be mad or upset. It's just something that happened…something we couldn't deny."

"Are you in love with my daughter?"

"Yes. Surely this is what love feels like."

Loraine smiled sweetly. "Then that's good enough for me."

"There's just…one other thing." She felt tears in her eyes and she blinked them away. "The night I got pregnant…"

Loraine nodded. "That was the night Matt died."

Annie let her tears fall. "Yes. I'm so sorry."

CHAPTER THIRTY-EIGHT

Annie came in carrying bags, and Jordan hopped up to help her, surprised to find her mother coming up the steps after Annie, carrying as many bags as Annie was.

"Did you buy the store out?"

"I had the most wonderful time shopping," her mother said. "This one loves to shop. So unlike you."

"Well, glad she could indulge you," she said.

"It was fun," Annie said. She then shocked Jordan into a stunned silence by kissing her full on the lips. "Miss me?"

Jordan glanced quickly at her mother, who was watching her.

"Well? Did you miss her?"

Annie laughed. "She's so cute when she blushes."

Jordan looked from one to the other. *What the hell is going on here?*

"Yes, she is." Her mother held up the bags. "So which bedroom should I put these in?"

"Follow me," Annie said.

Jordan rubbed her face with both hands. Jesus...God... Annie *told* her? She stumbled into the kitchen and pulled down the twenty-year-old bottle of scotch she'd been saving for a special occasion. She'd dropped a hundred and fifty bucks for the Glenlivet, but it was without ceremony that she opened it now. Her hand trembled slightly as she poured a small amount into a glass. She barely took the time to savor the aroma of the liquid gold before drinking it.

"She kissed me in front of my mother," she whispered to the empty room.

She poured another splash into the glass, then closed the bottle. She heard their voices and turned as they came into the kitchen. Her mother's eyebrows rose.

"Kinda early for scotch, isn't it?"

"I...umm...no. No."

Her mother came closer and hugged her, then kissed her quickly on the cheek. "I love you, Jordan." She pulled away and looked at Annie. "Don't forget...dinner on Sunday."

"We'll be there."

Jordan watched as her mother hugged and kissed Annie as well, then left with a wave of her hand. Jordan set her glass down, her mind spinning.

"I adore your mother," Annie said.

Jordan blinked several times. "So...she knows?"

Annie smiled. "Yes, she knows."

"Did she freak out?"

"No. In fact, she already knew. I didn't have to tell her."

Jordan's eyes widened. "How?"

Annie shrugged. "Mother's intuition, maybe. Doesn't matter. We had a nice talk. I told her...well, I told her about that night with Matt. And then we had a good cry."

Jordan ran her hand through her hair. "I can't believe my mother knows." She glanced at Annie. "Old habit...but I don't normally expose my personal life to my mother."

Annie walked over to her, close enough for their bodies to touch. She met her eyes, then leaned closer and kissed her. "Your mother loves you, Jordan. No matter what. I didn't see the point in lying to her."

Jordan pulled Annie closer, relishing the embrace. "No, you're right." She kissed Annie gently. "But are you okay with her knowing? I mean—"

"I'm okay with her knowing." Annie pulled out of her arms. "This is all new to me, Jordan. But I don't feel I want to hide it. Do you?"

"What about your mother?" she asked.

Annie smiled quickly. "Now *that'll* be fun," she said sarcastically. "Can you see it?"

"She'll hate me."

"Oh, sweetheart, I hate to tell you this, but I think she already does."

Jordan stared at her. *Sweetheart.* Had she ever been called "sweetheart" before?

"What?"

Jordan smiled. "Nothing."

"Okay. So do you want to see what all we bought?"

"Sure."

Annie wiggled her eyebrows. "I'll model for you."

Jordan grabbed her hand and pulled her closer, kissing her. "Then you won't get past the first outfit."

Annie looped her arms around Jordan's neck, their kisses no longer gentle. "I'll let you help me dress."

Jordan smiled against her lips. "How about I help you undress?"

CHAPTER THIRTY-NINE

"So you're really leaving, boss?"

Jordan nodded. "Yeah. You know, I do have a real job."

Brandon wiped the blond hair off his forehead. "Gonna be kinda strange here without you."

"I'm trusting you to handle things," she said. "I *will* be back, you know."

"Annie's gonna be here though, right?"

"She'll be working part-time this fall. Come January, well, her baby is due then. She's also got student teaching lined up. So when she's not here, you're in charge."

Brandon lowered his voice. "I don't think your dad likes me."

Jordan laughed. "He thinks you're a hippie."

"A hippie? Really?" He laughed. "Cool."

"Just…don't do anything too crazy," she said. "I don't know when I can come back. I've got to get somebody else in here by January."

"You can trust me."

"I know."

She sat down behind the desk when he left. The office felt empty without Annie there. Jordan wondered how her first day back at school was going. She knew Annie didn't want to go, but she was so close to finishing, Jordan had told her the semester would fly by. But would it? Or would it crawl by?

She couldn't believe the summer was over, couldn't believe she'd be leaving in four days. The last two weeks had been a blur. She and Annie had tried to cram as much time together as possible. Other than dinner with her parents the one night, they'd spent every evening at home, sharing cooking duties and sharing stories. It was so easy being with Annie. They could talk for hours, like friends did. And they could make love for hours, like lovers did. There were never any awkward moments between them. It was too easy. How could she not fall in love?

Yet, Chicago was calling. Summer fun was over, and it was time to get back to her real life. She tried to tell herself that being apart from Annie would be good for both of them. Being in a relationship with another woman—it was all new to Annie. Separated, maybe Annie would take the time to fully evaluate it and decide if this is truly what she wanted out of life.

Jordan felt a tightness in her chest, a slight pain in her heart. What if Annie decided just that? That this wasn't what she wanted. What if she couldn't live with the thought of her mother finding out? Or what if with her being away, these feelings fled? What if—

"Stop it," she told herself.

She could go on for hours with "what-ifs" and it would solve absolutely nothing. She was leaving. She had accepted that. So had Annie, despite her tears.

She was leaving.

CHAPTER FORTY

Annie wiped at her tears, standing in the driveway long after Jordan's SUV had faded from view. She'd told herself she would not cry. At least, not in front of Jordan. But she felt like her heart was breaking, and she let her tears flow at will now.

"It'll be okay," Jordan had whispered.

"No. No, it won't be."

"I'm a phone call away."

Another hug…another desperate kiss…and Jordan was gone.

She looked down the lonely driveway. Yes, Jordan was gone. Oh, she promised she'd be back and Annie believed her. Didn't she?

Yes, of course she did. They'd made love with such abandon last night, as if Jordan was trying to imprint her touch on Annie's body. Jordan had loved her so thoroughly that Annie had been in a state of pure bliss by the time they had finally given in to sleep.

Being with Jordan was so different than Derrick, than Matt. Jordan was soft where they were hard. Jordan was slow where they were quick. Jordan was gentle where they were rough. And even though it could be slow and gentle, that didn't mean it wasn't intense and passionate too. It was.

So, yes, surely Jordan was coming back.

Annie felt a small smile tugging at her lips. She remembered Jordan kissing her belly—kissing the baby—telling him that she'd be back soon. Real soon.

But what was soon? A couple of weeks? A month? Two or three months? Her smile faded at that thought. Could she make it for two or three months without her? Again, that nagging thought that Jordan would disappear—that she would stay away like she used to do—was lingering in her mind.

"I love her."

Then why didn't you tell her?

Because she was afraid to, that's why. And without Jordan here, it almost seemed like a dream—this crazy, crazy summer. A glorious, delicious dream…but still only a dream. Did she really get pregnant? Did she really fall in love with a woman?

Yes and yes.

She took a deep breath and blew it out quickly. Yes and yes. She wiped her cheeks dry and turned, heading back inside the house. Her house now. Her lonely, empty house.

At least she had Fat Larry's. She had inventory and ordering to do this morning. Then she had two classes this afternoon. The day would pass by quickly, she hoped.

And instead of coming home to an empty house and a solitary dinner, she'd already made plans with Suzanne. Britney was going to stay with her grandmother, so they'd have the house to themselves. They were going to pick up Chinese food and watch a movie and catch up. Things would get back to normal.

Whatever normal was.

* * *

"You've been awfully quiet," Suzanne said as they cleaned up after dinner. "Is everything okay?"

Annie forced a smile. "Yes, of course."

Suzanne studied her. "I saw you last week and you were absolutely *beaming*. Today…not so much."

"Well, the fall semester started. I'm driving to Corpus three days a week now." Annie shrugged. "And still working at Fat Larry's as much as I can."

"So you and Brandon are really running things? How's that going to work out?"

"It'll be good. Brandon has grown up so much this summer. I think he likes the responsibility that Jordan has given him."

"Is she going to come back at all?"

"Yes. She says…yes."

Annie turned away. Could they talk about something other than Jordan and whether she would return to Rockport or not? Annie was feeling insecure enough as it was. She didn't need Suzanne putting more doubts in her mind.

Suzanne touched her arm. "What's going on, Annie?" she asked gently.

Annie bit her lip. "What do you mean?"

"You look like you're about to cry."

Annie closed her eyes for a moment. *Oh, crap.*

"Annie, what is it? Is everything okay with the baby?"

Annie touched her belly. "Yes, everything is fine with the baby. I'm getting huge."

Suzanne smiled. "You are not. Give it a couple more months before you say that."

"I know. I still have over four months to go."

"So what's wrong?"

Annie gave her a weak smile. "I'm…lonely."

"Lonely?"

Oh, hell. "I miss her." Annie looked at Suzanne. "She's only been gone one day and…and I miss her like crazy."

Suzanne frowned. "Jordan? Well, I guess you got used to having a roommate."

Annie hid her smile. "Yes. Something like that." She grabbed Suzanne's forearms and squeezed. "Listen, promise me you won't freak out."

"What are you talking about?"

God, this was probably a mistake but Annie so wanted to tell Suzanne what was going on in her life. She wanted to share that with Suzanne...with *someone*.

"Just promise me you won't freak out," she said as she released Suzanne's arms.

Suzanne nodded. "Okay, I won't freak out. But you're starting to scare me. What's going on?"

Annie took a deep breath. "Jordan and I...well...this summer..." She scratched the side of her neck nervously. "We're kinda...involved. Sexually."

Suzanne literally shrieked, then covered her mouth with her hand, her eyes wide with shock.

"Oh. My. God. You're having *sex* with her?"

Annie nodded. Okay, so maybe telling her wasn't such a good idea after all.

"Oh...my *God*. What did she do to you? Did she force you?"

"Of course not."

Suzanne stared at her. "Oh, my God. I can't believe it. She's a...a *lesbian*."

Annie nodded. "Yeah. That's kinda the reason."

"Oh, my *God*," she said once again. She shook her head quickly from side to side. "You have lost your freakin' mind."

Annie held a hand up. "You promised you wouldn't freak out."

"Yeah, but I didn't know *this* was what you were going to tell me." She shook her head. "How did this happen? I mean, I can't believe it. I just absolutely cannot believe it."

"Why can't you believe it? After everything I've told you about Derrick, about me not being interested in anybody, about how...bad it was when I slept with Matt. Why can't you believe it?"

"Yeah...but a *woman*?"

Annie went closer, taking her hands and squeezing. "Remember when you came over to the house that day we had the office party? And you caught me staring down at the pier? You thought I was staring at Brandon." Annie shook her head. "It wasn't Brandon I was staring at."

Suzanne's shoulders sank. "Oh, my God," she whispered. "I'm in love with her."

Suzanne shrieked again. "In *love*? With a *woman*?"

"Yes. Crazy in love."

Suzanne sank down into a chair at the breakfast bar, her head shaking slowly, back and forth. "In love?"

"Crazy in love," she said again. "I'm...happy, Suzanne. She makes me happy." Annie sat down next to her. "Remember that day we had lunch, when I asked you if you were happy being married? I told you I had never been. That's the truth. Living... being with Derrick, never made me happy. He tried...*I* tried, but I was never happy." She took Suzanne's hand once again and squeezed it. "Living with Jordan, being involved with her like I am, makes me so very, very happy. I won't blame you if you can't understand how I feel, Suzanne. But please, I just want you to be happy *for* me."

"I know. I know. It's just...I never expected this."

Annie tilted her head. "Didn't you? Surely you could see how close we were getting."

"Yeah. I thought, well, that you needed a friend is all."

Annie nodded. "I did. And she became a very good friend. But we were closer than that. I think from the moment we met, we were closer than that."

Suzanne ran a hand through her hair. "If you think Derrick flipped out over you being pregnant, this will send him over the edge."

Annie shook her head. "Hello? Divorced, remember?"

Suzanne smiled. "Hello? Derrick, crazy man, remember?"

Annie laughed. "I know it will be a shock to him, but I don't think he'll go crazy over it. I told you we had a good talk. He knows it's over with us."

"A small town like this," Suzanne said. "When people find out his ex-wife is now suddenly gay..." She paused. "That's what this is, right? Or is this just a phase or something?"

"It's not a phase, Suzanne."

"So you're...gay now? Or do you call it bi?"

"I don't call it anything. I call it being in love with Jordan."

CHAPTER FORTY-ONE

Jordan stared out the window, surprised at how claustrophobic she felt surrounded by high-rises in every direction. She tugged at the collar of her blouse, then shrugged out of her jacket and casually tossed it over the back of her office chair. She never thought she'd miss wearing shorts and Fat Larry T-shirts to work, but she did.

She again turned her gaze out the window, slowly shaking her head.

What the hell are you doing here?

Four days back, and she had a terrible ache in her heart. She was back in her old routine, she just never realized how *empty* it had been. There was a void in her life now, without Annie around. How had she lived so long without her? How had she lived so long without love?

"The New York office called," Peter said as he walked into her office. "Said you did a great job negotiating on the Dunbar contract."

Jordan turned from the window and shrugged. "Good."

"Good? That's it? You know they've wanted to move you there for some time now."

"Not going to happen," she said as she moved back to her desk.

Peter sat down across from her in one of her plush visitor's chairs. He folded his hands together, then tapped them on his thigh.

"What's going on with you, Jordan?"

She raised her eyebrows. "What?"

"It's like you're only going through the motions. You're getting results, but I don't see the same drive. Being away like you were...did you lose something?"

Jordan met his gaze. "No. I think...I found something."

"Are you burnt out? I know you put in an obscene amount of hours over the years. That takes its toll. I know. I did the same thing when I was your age."

She decided to be honest with him. Because, yes, she was just going through the motions with her job. Her mind wasn't here. Her spirit wasn't here. Her *soul* wasn't here. No, she seemed to have left that all behind in Rockport...with Annie.

"Being away as long as I was let me put things in perspective," she said. "And it made me realize how much I'd missed out on. Not only with my family, but with a personal life too. My focus was solely on this job, twenty-four hours a day." She leaned back in her chair. "I didn't realize how tired I was until I got away. Tired, both mentally and physically."

"So you've had a break," he said. "A nice long one. Is it going to take you a while to get back into the swing of things? I can shift some things around."

She shook her head. "I don't know if I *can* get back into the swing of things," she said. "My heart's not in it anymore, Peter. Like you said, I'm just going through the motions."

His eyes widened. "What are you saying? Are you thinking of leaving the company? My God, Jordan, do you know how many years you've invested in this? How many years *we've* invested in *you?*"

"I'm well aware of the hours I've put in, as are you," she said. "And leaving something that I've worked so hard for…that's not an easy decision."

"You'd really walk away from this? For what? To run a souvenir shop?" He laughed. "You can't be serious."

"I'm not happy here, Peter."

"No? You seemed to be happy enough when you left. What changed? You want more money?" He shrugged. "I can probably arrange that."

"It's not about money."

"Then what is it?"

"It's about…it's about life. And it's very short."

He sighed. "So your brother's death really had an effect on you."

"Did you think it wouldn't?"

"I thought you'd be over it by now and ready to get back to work." He stood up and glanced at his watch. "I have a meeting that I can't miss. But you need to let me know what you plan to do. I've got your schedule lined up for the next month already." He paused at the door. "Don't rush into anything, Jordan. We all go through stages of burnout. Hell, I've threatened to leave before myself."

She nodded. No, she wouldn't make an impulsive or hasty decision. She wouldn't have to. She'd been mulling it over ever since she stepped off the plane at O'Hare. She knew in her heart, the decision was already made. She knew before she'd even come back to Chicago, which made her question why she'd bothered to come back in the first place.

She picked up the phone before she could change her mind. It was her mother who answered her father's cell.

"Hey, Mom. Are you already getting ready for the dinner crowd?"

"We're still at the house. About to leave, though. Did you need to talk to him?"

Jordan hesitated. Was she being hasty? No. She kept seeing Annie's face, seeing the tears she had been trying to hide. No, she wasn't being hasty. She couldn't wait to get back home.

"Let me talk to him for a second," she said.

"Okay." Then, "Have you settled back in yet?"

"No," she said honestly. "I miss it there."

"We miss you too. Annie misses you."

Jordan laughed. "How do you know?"

"I talked to her this morning. She said you have only called once. She's afraid you're...well, that you're not coming back."

"I called and we talked for over an hour. And it made me miss her more so I haven't called again. Because...well, because if I call, I'll want to be there. Which is why I'm calling now."

"Oh?"

She smiled. "Let me talk to Dad."

"Okay, here he is."

"We're about to head to the restaurant, Jordan. What's up?" he said in a hurried voice.

"Remember when I told you that we'd need to hire a manager for Fat Larry's by January?"

"Yes."

"Well, cancel that. I'll be your manager." That statement was met with silence. "Dad?"

"You're going to come back? To stay this time?"

"If you'll have me," she said.

He laughed. "Pack your bags."

She couldn't keep the grin off her face. "You sure? You'll let me run the store?"

"Honey, I'll *give* you the store if it means you'll come back home."

She frowned. "Is that singing I hear?"

"Your mother is doing the happy dance and singing. Off-key, as you can tell."

She laughed. "Tell her not a word to Annie. I want to surprise her."

"I will. We love you, Jordan."

"Love you too."

Jordan spun around in her chair, taking in the view outside her windows again. She was smiling and she couldn't stop. Was it a hasty decision? Didn't matter. It was the right one.

She turned back to her desk and pulled her laptop closer. She pulled up her email, addressing one to Peter. Her fingers drummed the keys as she tried to decide what to write.

"It is with regret that I resign my position…blah, blah, blah," she muttered.

She deleted that as soon as she'd typed it out. No. No need to bullshit.

"I quit," she typed instead and sent it without a second thought.

She closed up her laptop and looked around the office. She had nothing personal here, not really. A few mementos she'd picked up on business trips but nothing that she couldn't live without. Well, there was the Petoskey stone she'd found in Michigan. She never had it polished, preferring to keep it in its natural state. She did on occasion dunk it in water to view the pattern on it. She picked it up and folded it in her hand, deciding it was something she wanted to take.

She looped her briefcase over her shoulder and headed to the door without looking back. She passed by Antonio's office and didn't bother to look inside. She did stop at Michelle's door, however. They'd worked together for years now, and they had a mutual respect for each other.

"Hey."

"Hi, Jordan. What's up?"

She smiled. "I wanted to say goodbye. It was a pleasure working with you."

She frowned. "You're leaving? You just got back," she said.

"Yes. I decided that I…well, that I need to be at home. With my family."

Michelle stood up and walked over to her. "So you're leaving me with Antonio for good, huh?"

"Sorry about that."

Michelle stuck her hand out, and Jordan shook it. "Well, I enjoyed working with you too. I'll miss you." She paused. "Giving notice or just up and leaving?"

"Up and leaving," she said.

"Don't you own a condo?"

"I do. It's in the Loop, Michigan Avenue. I shouldn't have a hard time getting rid of it."

"No, probably not."

Jordan nodded. "Well, good luck," she said and turned to go.

Perhaps it was rude not to say goodbye to the rest of her team, but she simply wanted to get out of there. She tapped her foot impatiently as she waited by the elevator. She wanted to get out of the city and go home.

Back to Rockport. Back to Annie.

And she couldn't get there fast enough.

CHAPTER FORTY-TWO

Annie leaned on the deck railing, watching the colors as they bounced across the water. It had been another gorgeous sunset, another one she'd viewed alone. She sighed and moved to where the ceiling fan was stirring the breeze. She couldn't decide when she missed Jordan the most. Was it now, sitting out here? Jordan loved the deck, loved sitting out and watching the water, watching the sunset. Or was it at night, in bed? Yes, she especially missed her there…missed sleeping with her, missed touching her, missed *being* with her. And she missed her at the store. Fat Larry's seemed empty without her there.

Her whole life seemed empty without Jordan around. How had that happened? How could Jordan come into her life so unexpectedly—so thoroughly—and disrupt her entire being? How could she have fallen so hopelessly in love with her in such a short time? But was it really that short? As she'd told Suzanne, from the first day they met, way back in early May, she'd felt something. She had been falling in love with her and she hadn't even realized it.

Her phone rang and she pulled it out of her pocket, smiling. Jordan had perfect timing.

"Hey," she answered.

"Hi. What are you doing?"

"Leaning on the railing, thinking about you," she said.

"Oh, yeah? I wish I was there."

"God, I do too," she said. "I miss you so much, Jordan."

There was only a slight pause as Jordan cleared her throat. "All this, Annie…it's been a mistake. A huge mistake. I'm sorry."

Annie felt her throat close up. "A mistake? Jordan…no. Please don't," she whispered. "I…I *need* you."

"Oh, honey, no," Jordan said hurriedly. "No. Not you. Not *us*. I meant here…Chicago. It was a mistake to come back."

Annie sank down into a chair. "Jesus, Jordan, you scared the crap out of me. I thought you meant—"

"I'm sorry. No. What I meant was…well, I miss you too. I'm coming home."

Annie gasped. "Home? You're coming home? Seriously?"

"Yes."

Annie squeezed her eyes shut. "For good?"

"For good."

Annie let out a relieved laugh. "You're coming home."

"You want me to, right?"

"God, yes. But what about your job?"

"I kinda quit."

"You quit?"

"Yeah. I heard there's an opening for a manager at Fat Larry's."

Annie laughed with delight. "I bet you have a good chance of getting it." She couldn't keep the smile off her face. "I can't believe you're coming back."

"Happy?"

"So happy. It's not the same here without you."

"No?"

"No. Empty." She paused. "And I missed you so much."

"Annie…I love you. I want to come back and make a life with you and the baby."

Tears filled Annie's eyes as she nodded. "I love you too."

"Is that a yes?"

Annie smiled through her tears. "Yes. Yes."

CHAPTER FORTY-THREE

Jordan paused at the door to Fat Larry's. She could have gone in the back, but...well, she wanted to see it, feel it and absorb it. Her store now.

She opened the door, smiling as the bell chimed her arrival. Brandon turned, a grin forming as soon as he saw her.

"Boss? What are you doing here?"

She smiled back at him. "What can I say? I missed you."

"Missed Annie, more likely," he said. "She's been moping around here lovesick since you left."

She raised an eyebrow. Were they that bad at hiding it?

He laughed. "Oh, come on. We're not blind."

"Does Annie know you know?"

He shook his head. "Don't think so."

She leaned closer. "Molly knows too?"

"*Everyone* knows."

She smiled. "Well, then I won't pretend that she's not the reason I came back." She glanced to the back. "Is she in the office?"

"No. Lunch. Suzanne came by." He looked at his watch. "Forty-five minutes ago, so she should be back soon."

"Okay. Well, I'll go see how messy my office is then."

He stopped her with a hand on her arm. "Glad you're back. Gonna stay a while?"

She nodded. "Yeah. I'm going to stay."

"Good. Because I didn't like having to get on Jessica for being late to work."

Jordan laughed. "You better let her know I'm back then. I'd hate to have to fire her."

She stopped at the popcorn machine and filled a sack, then grabbed a water bottle before heading into the office. It was neat and tidy, and she sat down, still smiling as she nibbled on popcorn.

Her flight hadn't been until later, but she'd gotten to the airport early, hoping to fly standby. She lucked out and got on the next plane out. It was a direct flight to Houston and she'd only had to wait a little over an hour before taking a commuter plane to Corpus. She'd left Chicago in a rush and had only briefly spoken with a real estate agent. He'd wanted her to hang around a few more days so they could meet and discuss the condo. No, hanging around wasn't an option. She'd have to make a trip back to settle things there and to make arrangements for moving her things down here. But that would have to wait. She simply couldn't stay there another minute.

Really, she didn't know how much of her stuff she wanted to keep, anyway. Her bed, for sure. She had a couple of pieces of furniture that she wanted to keep too. Her clothes? No. She would have no use for them here.

The back door burst open, and Annie stood there, staring at her, a smile on her face. Then she walked slowly into the office, pausing to close the door and lock it.

"You're early," she accused.

Jordan shrugged. "A little."

"A lot."

Jordan stood, smiling too. "I got here as fast as I could."

Annie finally came closer, falling into her arms. They kissed, hard, then softer, slower. Jordan pulled her as close to her body as she could, feeling the baby between them. She closed her eyes as Annie buried her face against her neck.

"I missed you so much," Annie murmured. "Please don't leave me again."

"I won't. I couldn't stand being away from you," she admitted. "I shouldn't have even tried."

Annie pulled back, meeting her eyes. "I love you."

"I love you too," she whispered.

Annie nodded and smiled. "Can we go home?"

"I thought it was your night to close."

"I'm fairly certain Brandon can be bribed to stay late."

Jordan kissed her quickly. "He knows about us, by the way."

Annie tilted her head. "Really? Good. Then I can quit trying to hide it."

Jordan kissed her again. "Apparently, you haven't been doing a very good job of it. Even Molly knows."

Annie's expression turned serious. "I'm glad they all know, Jordan. It feels so...so *real*, so special. I don't want to hide it. Not from anyone. I hope that's okay with you."

Jordan nodded. "Yes. Whatever you're comfortable with, I'm okay. But your mother may find out," she warned.

Annie nodded. "And I'm okay with that too. I love you. I don't care who knows."

Jordan pulled her into a tight hug, feeling as...well, as happy as she could ever remember. Annie made her feel whole and complete, made her entire existence on this earth meaningful. Finally, she felt at peace...and at home.

"Let's go home. I kinda missed Pelican's Landing too."

CHAPTER FORTY-FOUR

"It's a boy!"

Jordan went to her mother and hugged her. "It's a boy," she said again. "And he's beautiful."

Her mother started crying immediately, like Jordan knew she would. Even though her mother had not voiced her preference, Jordan knew she would be pleased if it was a boy. She glanced over at her father, who was beaming, and she went to hug him too.

"How is Annie?" her mother asked as she wiped at the corner of her eye. "She wasn't in labor too long. I hope she—"

"She did great," Jordan said. "It was the most amazing thing I've ever witnessed." Then she laughed. "And now I know that I don't ever, *ever*, want to give birth."

Her mother laughed. "No, honey, I can't see you pregnant."

"Let me get back in there," she said. "I'll come get you as soon as Annie is ready for visitors."

Her mother stopped her. "Jordan...what about Annie's mother?"

Jordan shrugged. "I called her as soon as we got here."

Her mother shook her head. "I just don't understand her. That's her grandbaby."

"I know, Mom."

"I feel so sorry for Annie."

"Me too. But she has you. That means a lot to her," Jordan said. "I'll be right back."

When she went back into the delivery room, Annie was still holding the baby and a nurse was supporting his head.

Annie glanced at her and smiled. "We're learning how to breast-feed."

Jordan stopped. "Ah…maybe I should, you know, come back later."

Annie laughed. "Come over here. You made it through the birth, I think you can make it through this."

Jordan smiled. "He's so damn cute," she said as she walked closer. "I can't believe how much hair he has."

"Look at him latching on already," the nurse said. "You won't have a problem with him nursing."

"That's so beautiful," Jordan whispered. She met Annie's gaze. "You're both so beautiful."

Annie reached a hand out and tugged her closer. She glanced over at the nurse. "Thank you."

The nurse smiled and left them alone. Jordan squeezed her hand tight. "I love you, Annie."

"I love you. And we have a family now."

"Yes, we do." Jordan leaned closer and kissed her. "How do you feel?"

"Tired. But happy. I imagine your parents are anxious to come in, huh?"

"Whenever you're ready. Do they need to take him to the nursery?"

"After we breast-feed, they'll take him for a bath and an examination. I'll move to the maternity ward then."

"You want me to tell Mom to wait?"

"Oh, no. She can come in and see him before they take him." Annie smiled. "We can't keep saying 'him,' you know."

"Have you decided on a name?"

"I liked the one you picked," Annie said.

Jordan smiled. "I picked a new favorite every week. Which one?"

"Jacob Matthew Thomas Sims."

Jordan grinned. "Jake. I picked that name last week."

"Yes. I love it. Do you think your mother will?"

Jordan nodded. "Yes. She'll be thrilled."

Annie's gaze was locked on the baby. "Your mother said that both you and Matt were born with hair like this," she said. She brushed her fingers gently through it. "I love that he's so much like you."

"Annie...I'm sorry that your mother is not here."

Annie looked at her quickly, then turned her gaze back to Jacob. "I know. I thought that she...well, I thought that she might come by. Maybe she'll wait until we get back to Rockport."

"Honey, give her time. She'll come around."

"You keep saying that. But so far—"

"How can she not? Look at him? He's so beautiful. She'll fall in love with him."

"I hope so." Annie drew her down for a kiss. "Why don't you go get your parents? I think I'm ready." She pulled a sleeping Jacob from her breast. "I think he's ready."

* * *

Annie woke slowly, rolling her head to the side. When she opened her eyes, Jordan was there, watching her.

"Where's Jacob?"

"Sleeping," Jordan said quietly, motioning to the crib beside her. "He's adorable."

Annie smiled. "You're adorable." She sat up. "How long did I sleep?"

"A couple of hours."

"He'll be ready to eat soon."

"Yes. Are we supposed to wake him to eat?"

"If he doesn't wake on his own, yes," she said, trying to remember everything she'd learned. "For the first couple of weeks, he should feed every two to three hours."

Jordan took her hand. "How do you feel?"

"Better." She raised an eyebrow. "Have you eaten?"

Jordan shook her head. "No. I didn't want to leave you. Are you hungry?"

"Not really. But you should go get something. I'll be fine."

Jordan stood up, then leaned down and kissed her. "I love you. I'll be right back."

Annie smiled as she watched Jordan leave, then her gaze drifted over to a sleeping Jacob. He was wrapped up tight in his blanket, his dark hair covered with a cap. She reached out and pulled the crib closer to her bed. She would let him sleep another halfhour before she woke him. She leaned back on her pillows, still smiling as she stared at him. He really was beautiful. She'd told everyone she didn't have a preference—boy or girl—but secretly, she'd hoped it would be a boy. She also knew Loraine wished for a boy. Not that Jacob could ever take Matt's place, but he would at least be a tiny replica of his father.

She turned to the door when she heard a light knocking on it.

"Come in," she called. She was surprised to see her mother open the door.

Her smile faltered a little as her mother came into the room. She wasn't sure what to say to her. Their relationship had deteriorated even further, and Annie hadn't seen or talked to her in over a month. Christmas had come and gone without so much as a greeting. Even with all of that, she still expected—hoped—that her mother would show up for the birth.

"Are you okay?"

Annie nodded. "I'm fine."

Her mother's gaze slid to Jacob. "A boy?"

"Yes."

Her mother came closer. "What did you name him?"

"Jacob Matthew," she said.

"He looks beautiful."

"Yes. I'll wake him soon. He needs to eat." She smiled. "My breasts are huge. They're going to show me how to use a breast pump."

Her mother finally looked at her, meeting her eyes. "I'm sorry I wasn't here."

Annie shrugged. "Loraine was here. And Jordan, of course."

She noticed her mother's expression harden at the mention of Jordan's name. She had yet to tell her mother the extent of their relationship. She could only imagine her reaction. She feared it would drive a permanent wedge between them and she wasn't ready for that. She hoped that the baby could bring them closer together again.

"Are you going to continue to live there? With her?"

"Yes."

"You're going to need help, Annie. You could come home with us," her mother offered.

Annie tilted her head. "Mom? During my whole pregnancy, you've been ashamed of me. I know at the beginning, it was a shock to you. But after all this time, you've still remained distant. Why is that?"

"I think maybe it is you who has been distant."

Annie shook her head. "No." She paused. "Is all of this really because I'm living with Jordan?"

"You know how I feel about her."

"Yes, you've made that perfectly clear. The problem is, you don't even know anything about her. She's...she's so kind and caring. She's...she's solid. No matter what, she's been there for me. Through all of this, from the first day I met her, she's been my rock. I don't think I could have made it through this without her."

"You don't have to try to sell her to me, Annie. I simply don't approve of her lifestyle." She pointed at Jacob. "And now you're going to expose an innocent baby to all that. God only knows how he's going to turn out."

Annie bit her lower lip, trying so hard to keep her retort inside. She failed, however.

"Turn out?" she asked loudly. "Children of gay parents turn out perfectly fine, thank you. He will have a very loving home. And he will have grandparents who love him and spoil him." She paused. "Well, at least one set, anyway."

"You act like I don't want to have anything to do with him."

"Do you? You don't want to have anything to do with me."

"Nonsense. If that was the case, I wouldn't have offered for you to move back with us." She took a step closer. "Please consider it, Annie. If not for you, then for the baby. He needs a *normal* home. You don't know what she might do to him."

"Oh, God, I can't believe you just said that."

"It's the truth. You don't know. She could—"

"Stop it," she said. "Please don't say something you're going to regret."

"Regret?"

"Yes. Because Jordan and I are—"

She stopped when the door opened, relieved to see Jordan there. Jordan paused when she saw her mother, but Annie waved her in.

"Hello, Mrs. Thomas," Jordan said with a smile. "Glad you could make it by." If Jordan noticed the tension between them, she didn't acknowledge it. Instead, she handed Annie a plastic wrapper. "Cookie," she said.

"Thank you." Annie looked up at her mother, seeing the scorn on her face as she avoided looking at Jordan. Annie had had enough. She took Jordan's hand and smiled as Jordan's eyebrows shot up. "As I was saying, Mom...Jordan and I are more than friends." Her mother looked at her sharply. "I love her."

Her mother gasped and held a hand to her chest. Her eyes went between them, landing on their clasped hands. Annie was shocked by the rage she saw on her face. Her mother turned to Jordan.

"What have you done to her?"

Jordan's expression softened, and she smiled slightly. "I fell in love with her. That's all."

Her mother shook her head violently. "No! No. This is outrageous." She turned to Annie. "You will come home with me. I won't have you—"

"Mom, stop." Annie held her hand up. "I'm happy. For the first time in my life, I'm happy with someone. This is who I am."

"No! This is *not* who you are. Not *ever*, do you hear me?"

"I'm sorry," Annie said. "But yes, this *is* me."

Their loud voices apparently roused Jacob from his sleep and his face turned red before he let out a cry. Jordan scooped him up and held him for a moment, then gently handed him over to her.

"He's hungry," Annie said. She unbuttoned her gown and her mother turned away from the sight of her breasts.

"Mrs. Thomas, I'm sorry that you don't understand this love between us," Jordan said. "But it's real. I love your daughter very much and I only want to make her happy. That's my goal. To love her and make her happy."

"You can't possibly know—"

"I know I love her. I know she loves me. Nothing else matters."

Annie watched Jacob suckle her breast while she listened to their exchange. She was surprised her mother hadn't already walked out.

"What about him?" her mother asked, pointing at Jacob.

"We're a family now," Jordan said. "He will have plenty of love."

"He needs a father."

"Well, he'll have two moms instead," Jordan said. "And I hear Derrick has offered to teach him how to play baseball," she said, surprising Annie. "I happen to have taught Matt how to play, so I'm pretty good myself. And then there's Brandon. He's our water expert. Swimming and sailboarding are already on his list." Jordan shrugged. "My father, of course, plans to be very active in his life. He'll have plenty of male role models."

Annie watched her mother closely, reading her expression. She knew exactly what her mother's next words were going to be.

"So…Derrick will be involved?"

"She said Derrick has offered his baseball expertise, that's all," Annie corrected. "Please don't take that to mean Derrick and *I* will be involved."

"And does he know about…well, this *change* in you?"

Annie smiled. "No. I haven't seen him in a while. I hear he's got a girlfriend."

"Really? But I thought—"

"He's not holding out for me, Mom. I told you, Derrick and I talked."

Her mother rubbed her forehead. "I don't understand all of this." She looked at Jordan. "I knew she shouldn't have ever moved in with you in the first place. Then this wouldn't have happened. I tried to warn her."

"It still would have happened," Annie said. "I love her, Mom. I want you and Dad to be a part of my life, a part of Jacob's life. But just know that Jordan is a part of that too."

"You think I can accept this? Accept that my daughter is having an affair with a woman?"

"It's not an affair," Jordan said.

"And what do *your* parents think about this?"

Jordan shrugged. "My parents love me, they love Annie. They don't try to interfere."

Her mother shook her head. "It's just such a shock. First, the pregnancy. Now *this*? It's like I don't even know you anymore."

"Then get to know me, Mom. Once we're settled, come by the house. Loraine is going to stay with us for a few days, until I'm comfortable with him on my own."

"She is?"

"Yes. I'd like for you and Loraine to get to know each other better too. She's a wonderful person, Mom."

Her mother hesitated a moment. "I suppose I could come by. Your father will want to see Jacob, of course."

Annie nodded. "Good. I'd like that."

Her mother cleared her throat. "Well, I should probably get going." She walked over to the bed and touched Jacob's head. "Looks like he took to breast-feeding easily."

"Yes." Annie grabbed her mother's hand. "Thank you for coming by."

Her mother nodded. "I'll...I'll call you in a few days. We'll come by to see you." Her mother turned to Jordan. "And we'll see you too, of course."

Jordan smiled. "Looking forward to it."

CHAPTER FORTY-FIVE

Jordan turned as Annie came out on the deck. She was carrying a bottle of wine and two glasses.

"Escaped, did you?" Jordan asked.

"He's in good hands, I think."

"Are they arguing over who gets to feed him?"

Annie smiled. "They're telling stories about when we were babies." She poured wine into the glasses. "I'm glad I'm not breast-feeding anymore. That pump was a bitch."

Jordan laughed. "Thankful for small breasts after all, huh?"

"Oh, I'm glad I got to experience breast-feeding, but I'm not that disappointed that I couldn't produce enough milk for him." She held her glass up and touched Jordan's. "Besides, now you don't have to drink alone."

Jordan moved away from the railing and into the shadows, pulling Annie with her. She leaned closer, kissing her lightly. "While I'm glad our mothers are getting along, I miss *us*."

"Yes, it seems that one or the other is always here."

"Your mother has actually been civil to me," she said.

"I noticed that. She also saw us kissing and didn't freak out."

Jordan nodded. "My mother kinda had a talk with her," she admitted.

Annie pulled back. "Really? Giving her advice on having a lesbian daughter?"

Jordan laughed. "Something like that." She kissed her again. "So can I be rude and tell them not to come over every day?"

Annie nodded. "Yes. I think three weeks is long enough. But maybe you should let me tell them."

"Here's an idea. Let's have everyone over for dinner Sunday. We'll tell them how grateful we are for their support and assistance, but that we're ready to be on our own. Short, sweet and to the point."

Annie set her glass on the railing and looped her arms around Jordan's neck. "Sounds like a plan. Because I miss you sleeping naked."

Jordan smiled against her lips. "Oh, honey, there's a whole bunch of things I miss."

Annie pulled back, her expression turning serious. "I love you, Jordan."

"I love you too. We're going to have a great little family."

"Yes, we are."

Annie leaned in to kiss her, their playfulness of earlier vanishing as their kiss deepened. Jordan pulled her closer, relishing the full-body contact that had become impossible while she was pregnant.

"*Oh…my.*"

They pulled apart guiltily at the sound of Annie's mother's voice. Neither of them had heard the door open. Annie squeezed Jordan's hand briefly.

"Is he sleeping already?"

"Yes. I was about to head out. I'm sorry…I didn't mean to—"

"Mom, it's okay. We just haven't had much alone time." Annie headed to the door. "I'll see if Loraine needs any help."

Jordan nearly panicked as Annie left her alone with her mother. Not freaking out when seeing them share a tiny kiss was not the same thing as seeing them in a passionate embrace. Annie's mother was the first to break the silence.

"Loraine told me that you and Annie…well, that your relationship was like any other. I still had a hard time comprehending it though."

Jordan walked closer. "I'm sorry. We should have been more considerate of you."

"No. This is your home," she said, surprising her. "Seeing you like that," she said, motioning to the shadows where they'd been, "makes me realize that you really are in love with each other."

"Yes, we are."

"I always knew Annie was never really happy with Derrick. I think I knew before they even got married. I should have said something to her, but…well, I thought Derrick would be good for her." She turned to face Jordan. "I see now that she is truly happy…with you. I'm sorry for the way I acted."

Jordan shrugged. "I appreciate that. But you should apologize to Annie, not to me."

She nodded. "Yes. I should." She moved away. "Well, I need to get going."

"Thank you for your help, Mrs. Thomas. It means a lot to Annie."

She paused at the door. "Jordan…please call me Clara."

Jordan smiled. "Thank you. I will."

* * *

"He looks just like Jordan."

Annie smiled. "Loraine, he looks like Matt."

Loraine laughed. "Well, Matt and Jordan looked alike."

Annie went over and hugged her. "It's okay to say he looks like Matt."

Loraine sighed. "I miss him so much sometimes."

"I know."

Loraine sighed again. "Well, this little fella is going to be spoiled rotten, I can assure you that."

"I have no doubt," she said with a laugh.

"Where's Jordan?"

Annie laughed. "I left her out on the deck with my mother. She caught us kissing."

"Oh, poor Jordan."

"Poor Jordan what?" Jordan asked as she came into the room.

"I was telling her my mom caught us kissing."

"Yeah, thanks for leaving me out there," she said.

"What did she say?"

"She said she could tell that we were in love."

Annie's eyes widened. "She said that? My mother?"

Loraine laughed. "Not to embarrass you, but she did ask me how you...well, managed things."

"*Things*? Oh my God. Like *sex*?"

"Yes."

Annie covered her face with her hands. "Please say the two of you are *not* discussing our sex life."

Jordan laughed. "How could you possibly explain it to her? Do you even know?"

Annie held up both hands. "Stop it. Both of you. We're *not* having this discussion. *Ever*."

"Well, it wasn't like I went into details," Loraine said. Then she winked at Jordan. "Much."

Annie pointed at the door. "Out. Both of you."

Jordan laughed. "Come on, Mom. How about a glass of wine?"

"Sure. And I should call your father."

Jordan turned back around, a smile still on her face. "Come join us?"

Annie nodded. She took one last look at Jacob, then linked her arm with Jordan. "I adore your mother, you know. But I'd really like it if she and my mom would not discuss lesbian sex."

Jordan leaned closer and kissed her cheek. "You said you wanted your mother involved in your life."

"Funny," she said dryly.

"By the way, your mother said I could call her Clara."

"Oh, my God. What has happened to her? It's almost as if she *likes* you."

Jordan nodded. "I told you she'd come around."

Annie stopped. "Yeah, you did, didn't you?" She leaned closer and kissed her. "Thank you. You always make everything okay."

"I didn't do anything, Annie. Your mother knows you're happy. She can tell. Despite everything, that's all any mother wants, isn't it? For their kids to be happy?"

Annie met Jordan's gaze. "Yes. It just took her a long time to realize that." Annie kissed her again. "You're the best thing that's ever happened to me, Jordan. I love you so much."

Jordan didn't say anything as she pulled her into a tight hug. They stood that way for a long minute, holding each other, talking without words. It was new to Annie—being able to communicate with someone this way. Then Jordan loosened her grip and Annie pulled away.

"Just so you know," Jordan said. "I never thought I could be in love like this. I sometimes wonder if I'm not dreaming all of this."

Annie smiled. "If it's a dream, then please don't wake me up."

Bella Books, Inc.

Women. Books. Even Better Together.

P.O. Box 10543
Tallahassee, FL 32302

Phone: 800-729-4992
www.bellabooks.com

CPSIA information can be obtained
at www.ICGtesting.com
Printed in the USA
JSHW081725150723
44822JS00001B/2